Star
(Psi Cassiopeia)

Star
(Psi Cassiopeia)
*The Marvelous History
of One of the Worlds
of Outer Space*

by
C. I. Defontenay

adapted by
P. J. Sokolowski

A Black Coat Press Book

Acknowledgements: We are indebted to Marsha Jones at DAW Books and Samuel T. Payne.

Original English translation Copyright © 1975 by DAW Books.

Revised English translation Copyright © 2007 by Black Coat Press.

Introduction Copyright © 1975 by Pierre Versins; translation Copyright © 1975 by Stanley Hochman.

Cover illustration Copyright © 2007 by Guillermo Vidal.
http://www.gevidal.com.ar/webdocses/catalogo.htm

Visit our website at www.blackcoatpress.com

ISBN 978-1-932983-99-9. First Printing. July 2007. Published by Black Coat Press, an imprint of Hollywood Comics.com, LLC, P.O. Box 17270, Encino, CA 91416. All rights reserved. Except for review purposes, no part of this book may be reproduced or transmitted in any form or by any means, electronic or mechanical, including photocopying, recording, or by any information storage and retrieval system, without permission in writing from the publisher. The stories and characters depicted in this novel are entirely fictional. Printed in the United States of America.

Introduction [1]

I've always been irritated—but only a little, let's not exaggerate—by the chauvinistic attitude of Americans (the Monroe Doctrine forever!) toward foreign science fiction. Since I am French, I am particularly galled by their willful ignorance of what is happening and what has happened in French science fiction. Though there seems to be some improvement lately, the situation is such that it could make me chauvinistic in turn, and I wouldn't at all like that.

However, where *Star, or Psi Cassiopeia* is concerned, I can hardly reproach Americans with their ignorance since, until it was reissued in 1972 as part of the excellent *Présence du Futur* imprint by publisher Denoël, this Defontenay novel was completely unknown to the French themselves. Just think—in 1966, when I wrote a long analysis of it, only five copies could be found. Two were stashed in major public libraries and I own one of the remaining three.

As a matter of fact, it was at the Bibliothèque Nationale in Paris that Raymond Queneau [2]—who was studying literary oddballs and eccentric writers for a

---

[1] This foreword was written by French science fiction scholar Jacques Chamson, a.k.a. Pierre Versins (1923-2001) for the first American edition of *Star*, published by DAW Books (No. 167) in 1975, and was translated by Stanley Hochman. (*Note from the publisher.*)

[2] French poet and novelist (1903-1976) famous for his 1959 novel *Zazie dans le métro*, which was adapted into a film by Louis Malle in 1960. (*Note from the publisher.*)

monumental work that he never completed, but from which he drew the title of his novel *Les Enfants du Limon*—discovered *Star* in 1930. He mentioned it in a special 1949 issue of the *Cahiers du Sud* devoted to "Minor French Romantics," praising both the author's thematic ingenuity and his style, which certainly has aged better than some passages from Victor Hugo. (It should probably be noted that the beginning of Defontenay's tale is in blank hexameters, a stylistic practice as uncommon then as it is now.)

On the other hand, the work was slaughtered in a short review by Camille Flammarion,[3] the well-known popular astronomer, at the end of that thematology of fictitious astronautics, his essay *Les mondes imaginaires et les mondes réels* (Real and Imaginary Worlds) (1864; reissued in 1877): "The supposition [a multiple stellar system with inhabited planets] is not lacking in cleverness," he wrote, "but it is far from showing an astronomer at work."

An astronomer, no. But a scientist nevertheless.

Born in Cahaignes, in the Department of the Eure, in Haute-Normandie, on February 16, 1819, Charles Ischir Defontenay came from a family of anticlerical farmers.[4] In 1845, he became a doctor of medicine, his

---

[3] Prolific author (18432-1925) of more than 50 books, including popular science works about astronomy, as well as several notable early science fiction novels, such as *La pluralité des mondes habités* (The Plurality of Inhabited Worlds) (1862), *Lumen* (1867) and *La Fin du Monde* (The End of the World) (1893). (*Note from the publisher.*)

[4] According to Jean José Marchand, Defontenay's father, Jacques Isidore Defontenay, was a farmer and postmaster; his mother was Elisabeth Albertine Camel. Defontenay had a

thesis, *De la Phtisie tuberculeuse*, being published by Rignoux. The following year, under the name "Dr. Cid"—a pseudonym composed of his initials—he released a study which is still part of literature, *Essai de Calliplastie*, published by Moquet. It was reissued in 1849 under the more accessible title, *Le trésor de beauté* (The Treasure of Beauty).

In 1850, Defontenay married Clémence Marie Sidonie Roty, the daughter of an attorney, who passed away at age 27 in 1854, the same year when *Star* was published. The young couple had twins and Defontenay became assistant to the Medical Director of the Hospital of Andelys. That same year, there also appeared a work entitled *Etudes dramatiques*. It included four plays— *Barkokébas*, *Le vieux de la montagne*, *Orphée* and *Prométhée*—and, like the novel, it was published by Ledoyen. Defontenay died on September 4, 1856, at the age of 37 from stomach cancer.[5]

In addition to the already mentioned comments by Queneau and Flammarion, Jean-José Marchand, who unearthed just about all we know of Defontenay—and revealed it in two remarkable articles which appeared in *La Quinzaine Littéraire* Nos. 100 and 138 (August 1970

---

younger brother, Florimond, who became a farmer. (*Note from the publisher.*)

[5] Also according to Jean José Marchand, Defontenay, whose surgery was in St. Germain-en-Laye, outside Paris, had befriended a number of Parisian literary celebrities, such as Théophile Gautier and George Sand who, in 1865, wrote an interesting science fiction novel, *Laura, ou le Voyage dans le Cristal* (Laura, or The Voyage inside the Crystal), in which a young geologist mind-travels into a crystalline universe inside a gem and then embarks on a journey to reach the Center of the Earth. (*Note from the publisher.*)

and April 12972, respectively), before prefacing the 1972 reissue of the book—notes that Defontenay's *Star* was the subject of an article by Théophile Gautier [6] (on August 22, 1854), and of a brief mention by Charles Monselet in the 1857 edition of *La Lorgnette Littéraire*.

Without knowing Marchand's work, I myself presented a detailed analysis and description of *Star* in the magazine *Ailleurs* (Nos. 5-6, 1966), before devoting an article to it in my *Encyclopédie de l'Utopie, des Voyages extraordinaires et de la Science Fiction* (1972). And that's about all the comments that have been written about a work that I personally feel is one of the jewels of 19th century science fiction.

Just what is *Star*? Nothing less than the second science fiction "space opera"—the first, of course, being *The True History*, written by Lucian of Samosata in the second century.

Lucian's *Book One* draws us joyously and irresistibly into the midst of a gigantic space battle in which extraterrestrial creatures, each one more amazing than the next, come running from the very ends of the galaxy to help the Lunarians in their just struggle—is a struggle ever anything but just?—against the Solarians.

Never will I forget those "20,000 Lacanopteres," which are large birds covered with plants instead of feathers, and upon which were mounted the "Scorodomaques" and the "Cenchroboles." Nor am I likely to forget the "Psyllotoxotes of the Bear Star" and the 50,000 "Anemodromes," nor the "Aeroconopes," the "Strutholabanes," or the "Nephelocentaurs" of the Milky Way. I have dreamt of them. I still dream of them.

---

[6] Famous French poet, dramatist, novelist, journalist, and literary critic (1811-1872). (*Note from the publisher.*)

I am also not likely to stop dreaming of the marvelous "psargino," the animal about whom we are given a note worthy of a naturalist at almost the beginning of *Star*.

There have been similar treatments since, of course, notably in the work of Olaf Stapledon,[7] but let's not forget that date—1854. The author was a doctor, which no doubt explains why the "psargino" is so plausible that one expects to run into it on turning the pages of a zoology treatise.

And what about those "abares," those spacecraft of ultramodern conception? They might even have inspired H.G. Wells' "cavorite" in *The First Men in the Moon* (1901)—that is, in the unlikely event that Wells had heard of *Star*. What could be both more precise and better described than those ovoid vessels—note the form, remarkable for the period—equipped with an anti-gravity system on which no author has been able to improve until modern times.

In reading Defontenay, one occasionally feels that he was preceded by a whole school of science fiction—by SF anthologies, magazines and—why not?—fan publications; in short, by numerous writers whose works could have influenced him, for the reader will come across many inventions that were rediscovered afterward, often *long* afterward. And when one thinks that Defontenay pushed audacity in his epic—for it is an epic—to the point of providing samples of Starian poetry and theater!

---

[7] British philosopher (1886-1950) and author of several influential works of science fiction such as *Last and First Men* (1930), *Star Maker* (1937) and *Sirius* (1944). (*Note from the publisher*.)

In short, isn't it true that here, a little past the middle of the 19th century, we already had a completely finished model of the science fiction novel and universe? How right the author was to emphasize at the end of his work what there was about it that was "strange, new and uncreated until then."

Pierre Versins
Rovray, February 28, 1975

ORIGINS

I.

Dare!
Be aware
That the highest stair
Of the Himalayas here
Are before us... and India is there
Under our feet. Climb that stair.
Hold! Brahma, in the air,
Rises fair
There!

II.

And the Indian pointed out in a group of peaks,
Rising out of the mountains, the brow of sublime blocks.
Before them, each Mogol bows in reverence,
Believing he worships the steps of the Hindu Zeus;
For the traditions of Tibet and Arachosia
Teach that Brahma, following across India
The granite stairway of the long Himalayas,
From those rocks, would leap to the zenith at times.

III.

Without delaying we took the way
That the hand of my Indian guide indicated.

Without any doubt, the course of a day
Would bring us to the mountain he noted
  As the major goal of our long ascent.
Then, for some anxious moments, we crossed
  Several ravines on a dangerous route;
In time, as the day declined, we reached
  A fresh plateau dappled with verdure
  Where we had to spend the hours of darkness.
  When I had had a meager supper,
  I fell into the unconsciousness
Which often follows extreme lassitude,
In spite of the noise which sometimes raised fears;
For the howling wind in that solitude
Echoed through all the Himalayas.

IV.

When I awoke, the sun already illuminated
Asia far and wide. A pure and limpid light
Lengthened my view up to the magnificent horizon.
For from that smiling knoll amidst peaks set back to
  back
India was spread out, and before my eyes were retraced,
From the summit of the giant mountain to the borders of
  space,
The diverse stages of the rich regions from which I came
Exploring. First there were, in the distant infinity,
Rain forests where clumps of tropical palms shot up;
And then meandering fields, where the clustered villages
Seemed to us at that hour to make the pinnacles
Of the Indian temples shimmer so capriciously.
To the west, on the other hand, at the mountain's foot,
  sheer walls

Were seen with a vast abyss that was hollowed from the
   rock,
The half-opened casket where the pearl of Asia shone:
My eyes discovered Kashmir in the bosom of its valley.
Terror truly came to assail me when I measured,
In that moment, the immense depths, the great void
Accumulated beneath my feet in a two-month journey
Which saw the scaling of meridional slopes and, at last,
Of these plateau arranged like a wide monstrous
   stairway
In the long Himalayas. Then, for a moment I considered
What, in these great mountains shaped as pyramids,
Gave rise to the series of steps in Brahma's stairs to the
   sky,
Which here appeared to be cut to the measure of his
 strides.

V.

But soon the voice of my guide,
Who complained of the inactivity
   I displayed, made me decide
To end the slow and tedious journey
   Of which we had fixed the time.
We had started full of hope and warmth;
   Each would with a firm step climb
The rough, uneven slopes of that earth.
   A sharp cold chilled the winds,
And nevertheless the sun's radiant glare
   On our perpendicular heads
Looked down from the sky of brilliant azure.
   By impracticable roads,
Crawling and creeping, we then met

Formidable ice fields,
A triple rampart, forbidding assault
Of the peak where Brahma's abode
Is concealed from mortals, of that dreaded spire,
The highest point in this world
Till then touched only by divine power.

VI.

When I saw myself so high, lost in that desert,
At the heavenly confines of the earth and chaos,
I had wanted to retreat. The savage sanctity
Of those lofty summits froze all my bravery.
Then it seemed that our journey
Was an insult, an injury
To the powers of the sky which we had come to tempt
So close to their habitation . . . And I, bowing
To such majesty, I gave precedence
To him when I saw the audacity in his face.
Avidly, his eyes
Embraced the considerable space
Still separating him from the greatest heights
Of the known world; for never had a climber
Seen himself so near
To the lugubrious spire
Which Hindustan, from far, regards with awe.
With such a success, his mind,
Rejoicing was inflamed
And exalted with a desire of immense conceit;
He let pride persuade
Him to try the escalade
Of mountains whose heights soared into the unknown
"Poor trembling idiot!"

"Stay if it seems right,"
He said with disdain. "I'm going to the highest
        "Of this planet's summits
        "To penetrate the secrets
"With which the gods surround themselves. To grow
  greater,"
        "Isn't that the desire
        "Of man in all his career?
"The sky is there so close!... Yes, I want to come
        "To the supreme abodes,
        "To take away the enigmas
"Concealed in their midst. Who knows whether, like
  God,
        "I would know in totality"
        "Or become a deity!" [8]
"What a temptation! when the sky is so close
        "That there you might touch Heaven!"
        And scarcely had he spoken
These words, then he rushed up as if inspired.
        With sacrilegious force
        In those formations of ice
He cut a path. I followed with my eyes
        His sublime madness;
        Watching his progress
From below, I seemed to see him fighting, suspended
        On the flanks of angry Olympus,
        Like Prometheus.

---

[8] The Indians believe that one can rise, through good works or penance, to the point of becoming one of the Heavenly Powers, to the point of dethroning a god. (*Note from the Author*)

VII.

A smooth and almost vertical plane
        He defies;
As he slashes the wall, his step on the mountain
        Slides.
He clambers up... and I see his hand
        Near
Enough in a moment to grasp the sacred
        Spire!
Before he could take a step, in the air
        Occurs
The most ominous uproar; red lightning's glare
        Spurs,
On a flaming trail, a fiery cloud,
        Fires
That the rapid, avenging breath of a god
        Hurls.
What stone torn from the eternal dome
        Are you sending?
Your side is opening! ...a fragment of Heaven,
        Descending,
Breaks of Brahma's peak. The shattered summit
        Falls,
And the Indian, horror! thrown from the height,
        Rolls!

VIII.

The meteor explodes in fragments with the granite,
And the furious blocks, boating over my head,
Smashed the high glaciers with their debris.
Old nests of sandy eagles rolled in the torrents...

The avalanche poured down its rock and snow;
It struck and overturned everything as it roared.
Oh, I didn't see it pass in my direction,
For my eyes closed; but I felt a freezing breath,
A jet of convulsive air hiss in my ears...

Then, the uproar descending, it died away in the depths.

IX.

The next day,
Following again, but all alone, the way
Which from the summits of those mountains
Had to lead me back into the hot plains
Of India, deluged in abundant sun,
On a rocky knoll, I came upon,
Lodged in the midst of a mass of gray and white,
By the avalanche thrown to that point
A strange block of metal a dull and dark color.
Its ridges, blunted to an uneven contour,
Still bore on its rough, blood border
The crushed remains of living, quivering matter.
My wounded heart sadly recognized
In that stone a heavy shard
Of the flashing meteorite
That had struck the Indian attaining the limit
Which a god, the guardian of the heavenly land,
Had drawn with a thunderbolt between him and that
world.

DISCOVERY

I.

Despite my cold disgust for that hideous spectacle, curiosity still compelled me to examine the celestial object which might have been held, perhaps, by the very hand of Brahma, or at least had long wandered amongst the Heavens, borne by the raging tides of the sea of stars.

II.

I cleared away the snow in which lay that stone from the sky, and then I could see the micaceous slab of its side, with some rough spot of its broken edge decorated with the most vivid flecks of gold. And still clearing away the snow, I saw something strange! The profile, somewhat jagged, of the meteorite revealed the opening of an cavity in its mass—a regular hole, the missing part of which was undoubtedly among the fragments lost or disintegrated during its fall.

III.

The meteorite was hollow!

What was this rock escaped from the volcanoes of an unknown sphere? From whence did it come in this way? From the desertic mountains of the Moon? Or, driven from farther away by the twinkle of a star floating in the river of worlds? Did it, tired, choose this narrow globe upon which to take refuge?

Why these hollowed flanks, this cube-shaped hole with metallic insides shining in dark magnificence?

My mind was overwhelmed by uncertainties...

IV.

I continued clearing away the snow while searching around the meteorite.

I hoped that its scattered remnants, its debris, would finally tell me from what larger fragment of stone or structure, this object had originated...

But I the thing that had fallen from the sky was gone; its pieces had continued rolling and were now undoubtedly lost in the depths of some gorge.

V.

In following the fall of the debris, my foot came to strike against a resonant object. In the rubble lay a finely worked metal chest. Its cover, slanted like that of a large box, was embellished with bizarre figures.

VI.

On the deserted hills of the Himalayas, that foreign object concealed a mystery!

By studying the signs chiseled on the strange casket, I tried to discover the origin of such a treasure, momentarily forgetting the meteorite which had showed me its hollow inside only a few yards away.

VII.

Now, my anticipation grew more and more. I grasped my knife to break the seals that kept the lids of the chest together.

Another slight effort and the two plates came unfastened.

Still, I hesitated, for my heart was beating hard inside my chest!

What could be concealed in that object buried in the coldest region of the grand mountains of Asia, at the highest limits of the inhabited world?

Were these the golden vessels of the gods of Benares? The miter of a high priest of a temple of Buddha? Or the diamonds of the Moguls' throne? Tell me, land of Golconda, that hides in your bosom jewels all aflame, did I find the treasure chest where your greedy rajah placed his most sparkling carbuncles?

And the seductive spirit of the marvelous delirium of these gilded dreams—oh! for an instant I feared being blinded by the flame one ray of sunlight could bring forth from the fire of riches enclosed in my hand.

Nevertheless, in trying to expel those splendid chimeras from my soul, the place, the object and its appearance made me anticipate some rare treasure.

Shaking, I opened it.

VIII.

I found several books and a small number of papers

in manuscript form.

IX.

It was impossible for me to fathom the language of these writings. I did not recognize the signs of the language as those of one of the nations pivoting around the Himalayan mountains.

Uneasy and curious about such events and strange mysteries, I resolved then to take possession of the chest. It was a great resolution; for there, doubtless, I had an immense secret to discover.

X.

Before withdrawing, one last time, my gaze ran over that stark scene—for two days, two centuries, the solitary witness of my long anguish.

A shattered pyramid, the decapitated peak seemed to open to spill its snow down the mountains.

The meteorite lay there, its gaping cavity facing the chest lying next to my feet.

XI.

In closing the chest which I intended to carry, I thought I saw on one of its sides a splash of dark, dried blood similar in color to that I had observed on the celestial stone...

Shreds of flesh smeared the meteorite—could the Indian's blood have spurted out to such a distance?

THE STARIAN BOOKS

The downward slopes of the paths were still obstructed by heaps of snow and interrupted by reefs of small stones. Carrying the load I had taken on among the higher peaks of the mountain, I descended two days more before finally reaching the cave where the Indian guides customarily have climbers store the supplies which would otherwise burden them. I arrived there dying of hunger and fatigue, since I had nothing more in my bag than some dry crusts of bread I was forced to soften in melted snow.

I rested half a day, my mind still full of the scenes that, not long ago, had appalled me. I opened the chest which had come into my possession. It was made of precious wood, covered with an layer of chiseled metal. I pulled out some of the books and manuscripts it contained. They were not in Persian, nor Tibetan, nor Hindi, nor even Chinese or Sanskrit. The horizontal alignment and cursive style of the characters made them resemble more closely those employed by the European nations. Above all, the paper was of a closer and denser texture than I had ever seen before.

I thought myself on the trail of some great historical mystery or of an important diplomatic secret.

My journey home was accomplished in various steps with a few diverse incidents. I have no reasons to report any of these here.

Having returned to my studies, I found myself ever tantalized by that stack of documents written in a language unknown even to the most expert archaeologists and linguists.

I searched; I searched. Great was the attraction that drew me to fathom the meaning of those pages from which I could not take my eyes.

I had the courage to begin again, methodically, patiently, to do for that strange dialect the work of a Champollion.

After six months of research, I had discovered the documents' alphabet and finally could assemble and articulate the words. From that moment, I allowed myself neither intermission nor relaxation before being able to decipher the meaning of several passages of the manuscripts and, above all, the books, which seemed to me to contain an unknown history, an unknown science.

After two years of effort, attention, and study, I was finally initiated into the workings of that language and able to penetrate the secrets of its translation; for several days, my soul was a tumult of numberless doubts, agonies and hesitations.

As I fathomed the meaning of those works, a supreme vertigo made me breathless.

Judge for yourself...

Avidly, I searched some passages of the books for anything I could relate to my everyday life; always interpreting, always translating, I found no mention of mankind or of things from this world. There was no evocation of sciences, customs and details similar to the sciences, customs and details of our world. What I was unraveling, through my studies, was the history and knowledge of a world to which ours appeared unknown.

Then, I remembered the circumstances in which I had discovered the chest, in the solitudes of the Himalayas, stained with the blood of the Indian crushed by the meteorite's fall; that celestial stone which, in breaking apart, had revealed an interior cavity, its other half undoubtedly lost forever in the snows of the mountain. Ah! I could no longer doubt it—the chest I had found only a few feet away from the meteorite had once been kept within it. My ambitious delirium had made me anticipate the discovery of a treasure inside that metal box—but what it contained was a whole new universe.

I quickly wished to discover to what intelligent being these books had once belonged, upon which celestial body—of which the meteorite had undoubtedly been a detached part—he had once stood and, above all, whose hands had written those manuscripts, which I had already recognized to be, for the most part, a selection from the correspondence of two friends, two sages.

Now, here is what an attentive reading of those papers taught me: the chest had once belonged to one of the highest civil officers of a great nation on one of those worlds which lit up the starry skies at night, scattered in the great void, in the immensity of the Heavens.

Far from the tumult and passions of his fellow beings, he had chosen to live a retired life in a retreat hollowed out of the rock of a mountain, which was occasionally shaken by volcanic earthquakes. There, in a niche cut into the porphyry of the rock, he usually placed in the chest his most cherished books and, above all, his most intimate thoughts recorded in a manuscript. I inferred from these details and circumstances that a crater must have opened in the part of the mountain where the sage's home was built and that, in a frightful eruption, its tongues of fire had thrown sections of the mountain an infinite distance into space.

Who could say how long those rocks had tossed about among the worlds, had remained wandering, until a powerful attraction, or a divine breath, came to launch them toward an obscure planet like ours—instead of the heart of a sun burning with fire?

It was only after consulting the astronomical and cosmographical charts contained in my interstellar discovery that I thought I could determine the position occupied by the star-sun whose satellite worlds I had begun to study. In the ocean of visible suns, the disposition and number of neighboring stars in the same plane led me to believe that it must be the star designated in the catalogs as Ψ in the constellation of Cassiopeia, that bizarre group of stars of which the five brightest mark the angles of an almost regular zigzag.

I have given that planetary system the name of "Star," which is fairly near the pronunciation of the word meaning "Earth" in the new language I had discovered.

It was expedient for me to collect in this book the substance of the Starian documents which I translated; perhaps you will find that I have done it with less method than imagination.

BOOK ONE

TAKING POSSESSION

I.

Beyond the orbits of Uranus and Neptune, higher than the region of the sky where Sirius blazes, menaced by the sword of Orion, fix your gaze on the line which runs from Polaris to Andromeda on the starred vault; transport your imagination to distances greater than several million times the distance from Sirius to the Sun—equal to an unlimited, almost infinite, number of times the distance from the Sun to the Earth—and, once that particle of the immensity of the Heavens has been glimpsed even imperfectly by your mind, go farther, farther still, ascend, ascend forever!... Perhaps then you will be able to reach in thought, in the depths of the constellation of Cassiopeia, a point perceptible through a telescope only on clear and calm nights. That point, that particle of light, is the star of the constellation which astronomers designate by the Greek letter Ψ and which, up there, the beings who think and speak call *Star*.

II.

In that vault of stars, in that sea of fires, which seems like so many candles destined to light our gaze as it plunges into the fields of infinity, Star is only a spark strong enough to send us a filament of light; but, up there, in the vast cluster where it displays its resplendence, that faint glimmer is a harmonious system of planets and satellites, the least of which is equal to ours in size and splendor.

III.

It was toward that point in space that I directed my thoughts, and, completely permeated by the reading and study of my Starian books, I crossed the Heavens faster than the speed of light; no longer did anything Terrestrial occupy my thoughts: I believed that I really was on a planet in the solar system of Star.

Frightened at first by the audacity of my project and by the immense void, the limitless solitude, which perhaps awaited me there, I anxiously searched for signs of the passage of some intelligent and sociable beings. I was soon reassured by the newly-acquired certitude that Nature, this sumptuous universe, would be neither rational nor complete if it was not inhabited by individuals capable of feeling and appreciating its poetic beauties; so I zestfully surrendered myself to the hope of admiring and living, in spirit at least, on that marvelous sphere.

IV.

It is done! In one leap, you have joined me in this new universe.

Yet, if, in that ethereal voyage we have just made across the incommensurable ocean of space, our thoughts, grazing in their flight the stars strewn along the way like so many luminous islands, could have stopped for a moment on a sun neighboring Star, they would have been struck by a singular fact. Among the millions of worlds the night shows us, hanging at various degrees in the sky, the planetary system of Star would appear as a graceful pleiad of multicolored suns and worlds and would still have been chosen from afar, for the exploration of those globes would seem to be supremely seductive and compelling.

V.

Now, we have descended onto one sphere in this system of globes; we are on an world warmed by its suns. Their heat is penetrating and inexpressible and their light soft and nuanced. And so, we propose to observe with pleasure, for here day—and even night—have a magnificence unknown to our eyes.

The region where we have set foot is rich and fertile, covered with close, vigorous, and exuberant vegetation. And it is on this dazzling life that we rest our eyes, when they are forced, though with regret, to turn to the sky, where four suns of diverse size and coloration, four bowers of celestial light, enamel the sky and sparkle from different points on the horizon.

VI.

Would that I could borrow the image-filled and sonorous expressions of the Starian language to describe the sky illuminated by its stars just as, in our Terran festivals, flashing jets of fireworks disperse in the air—the difference being that, on Star, each spark is a whole ball of fire!

VII.

The largest disc, the central pivot, the true sun of the Starian system, is named Ruliel. Its immense sphere, whiter than a trail of lightning, radiates a light so intense and so diffuse that the clouds cannot mask it entirely and its presence on the horizon attenuates the brightness of the other three suns.

At some distance from Ruliel, rises Altéther, with a surface and corona of transparent green. Altéther is the fine green sun which often accompanies Ruliel. It precedes it like a splendid, gentle dawn and, for some time thereafter, still pours its soft rays on the earth when the great star has already drowned its huge disc in the misty limbo of the west.

To the east, rises Urrias, the blazing red sun, the light of which, tampered by the fires of Ruliel, throws out a web of pale rose rays, which redden toward the far horizon. Urrias is the sun closest to the planet called Star and, as we shall see later, is one of its satellites.

Finally, we hasten to admire the last bright star of this magnificent firmament, for Erragror, the sun with a pure blue disc, is already preparing to set and bathes that part of the sky with its soft and melancholy light.

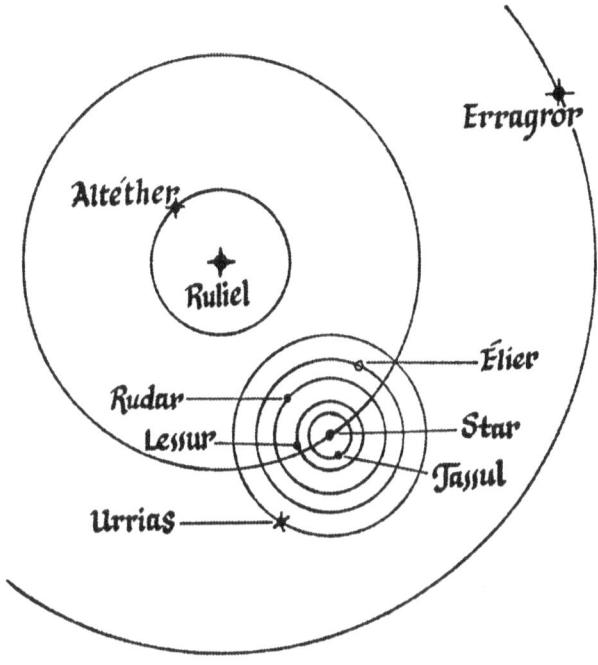

The Starian system

VIII.

We now lower our eyes to the earth, which the fires of its stars inundate with thousands of reflections, thousands of nuances of white and colored light. Another spectacle awaits us—a spectacle wonderful and sublime as a whole, but also admirably surprising in its details.

IX.

Vast forests are before us. Some birds hovering in the air first reveal the existence of living beings. Life and motion are already around us; we are no longer alone; but, above all, we want to find thinking beings... A curious eagerness makes us hurry irresistibly in search of humanity. What are the human beings of this world? What form, what bearing, what intelligence will they disclose to us? And our imaginations, traveling with us, have already endowed them with monstrous organs and fantastic powers.

X.

Advancing, we are surprised at the enormous variations presented by the planet's vegetation. Indeed, trees of terrific vigor rise like mountains, like superb peaks; and under their canopies, shading a circumference of more than a thousand feet, delicate plants of a glazed transparency and microscopic tenuousness spread out their filiform roots.

The tallest species of tree, which dominates the distant faces of forests and sinks deep, winding channels in them, is the *syphus*, an immense plant with a thousand boughs incessantly diverging and its highest branches lost in the clouds. There is nothing on this world comparable in size to the *syphus*, except a marine tree called the *tarrios*, which suspends vast forests over the liquid plains of the oceans.

XI.

The foliage of the *syphus* is of an orange color, softened by the velvet texture of the tips of its leaves; its flowers are clusters of delicate green. A generic uniformity of color is not found on this flourishing soil, either in the foliage of the trees or in the stems of the plants which cover it. Gray, blue, green and orange are the colors which most frequently clothe the leaves of plants; while the large and showy bowers are always in hues, contrasting with the foliage they accompany.

We say *contrasting* irrespective of the daylight that illuminates them, for we must not forget that, after the setting of Ruliel, the colors of the objects in the Starian world change from moment to moment, depending upon the blending or predominance of light radiated by the colored suns on the horizon.

XII.

We cross mysterious woods, where copses of trees, similar to green and yellow madrepores or other corals, raise to a man's height stone boughs covered with lovely blue flowers, as hard and unyielding as plates of ivory. This sort of forest coral seems to be a singular species of monocotyledonous tree, with an epidermis secreting a cuticle of very dense lime, which, drying in the air, envelops the trunk and branches like a sheath and gives the flowers the consistency, gleam and hardness of porcelain.

The wind claying through the branches of these trees produces metallic vibrations in chords following us with an aeolian and vaporous harmony.

XIII.

Our unforeseen arrival at the edge of a stream causes a strange tumult there. A multitude of shrubby trees with green, glossy leaves, surging up like birds, escape into the air, moving their branches and leaves in the manner of wings, and go to set themselves down on the basks, some distance away.

These bird-plants, named *bramiles*, are singular beings, which, with the structure of a plant, have the sensitivity of an animal and the ability to move by flexing branches jointed at the trunk. *Bramiles* fix themselves along the margins of streams by means of single tuberculate feet equipped with roots or claw-shaped suckers that they sink into the moist earth. Their gathering and the movement of their branches give a melancholy animation to the balks of the rivers where they live.

XIV.

Wishing to orient ourselves on this world unknown to us until now, we have climbed up the side of a high hill. Its summit is a promontory overlooking an immense sea. There, along its shores, are the *tarrios*, spreading out their crowns at water level and forming so many green islands lulled by the waves.

How many ideas of strength, majesty, and life rose up in us at the sight of these colossal trees, which, plunging their roots to the bottom of shallow seas or along its beaches, raise powerful limbs above the waves by means of enormous trunks capable of resisting the stress of tides and storms!

XV.

Imperceptibly, the suns have moved. Erragror has disappeared from the horizon, and Ruliel has followed it a short time afterward. Altéther itself shows its enlarged, green disc in the fluffy haze of the west. We have the privilege of seeing one of the incomplete nights of Star: while the multitude of far-away stars, eclipsed by the light of Ruliel, now become visible in the dark-blue sky, the five moons—or satellites—of Star appear, escorted by stars of the first magnitude.

But such nights, which have so many mysterious charms along the water, or in the forests that surround us, bring out splendors in the sky, and our fatigued eyes can no longer watch without resting for a moment.

XVI.

Star is the terrestrial globe, the inhabited and living sphere, the name of which has served us to designate generally the cluster of stars which we have entered.

Star is a planetary mass of ample volume, and its orbit occupies the intermediate position of the system, almost equidistant between Altéther, the green sun, and Erragror, the blue sun. Star, like these two suns, gravitates around Ruliel, immobile at the center of the system.

Around Star, or the earth, move five small globes, of which the farthest and most voluminous is Urrias, one of the four suns streaking across the sky. The other four satellites, destitute of their own light, appear as so many moons upon which to rest the eyes in a firmament full of blinding brilliance.

The first of these moons is named Tassul, the second is called Lessur, the third Rudar, and the fourth Elier. Such are, including the glittering strings of fiery stars, the riches of the night in this marvelous world.

XVII.

Star's twilights have a captivating magic. Despite the presence of Urrias and Altéther on the plane of the horizon, the disc of Tassul, illuminated in totality by the rays of Ruliel, rises clear and silver in the east. Lessur presents a strange phenomenon; half its surface, receiving the white light of Ruliel, is the pale yellow color of Tassul, touched with a nuance of blue, while the other half, reflecting only the rays of Erragror, presents a dim shade of blue. Rudar, on the other hand, lost amidst the red and green fires of Urrias and Altéther over our heads, suspends its crescent gleaming with chameleon colors.

XVIII.

The blue sun is already lost behind the western mountains. The red sun is also inclining toward that quarter, the tomb of all heavenly lights. For this earth, for these places always streaming with light, it is almost night—but a soft, tropical, and shimmering night.

At this moment, a singular star is rising in the blue of the opulent sky. Among the Starians, it is always contemplated with wonder. The people call it Elier. This satellite of Star is a diaphanous globe, solid and compact as an earth of crystal, but transparent as breathable air. Within the compass of the sky, where so many carbuncles shine as in a great casket, Elier is the diamond in which all the fires of suns, moons and stars play, cross each other and are reflected. As it advances, we see it project, in distinct, blazing rays, the colors of the rainbow. All the light of the suns, penetrating it together or one by one, spread out the blazing phantasmagoria of the refractible colors of the solar spectrum, or make warmly colored rings which ripple from the center of the star toward its circumference.

XIX.

What brush could render the different phases of the physiognomy of day or night under the enchanted sky of Star, wrought by the revolution of its suns and the unexpected changes taking place each moment in their respective positions? Who could describe, above all, the phantasmagoria of changing lusters these stars display in the waves of the sea, when they plunge into the water, trembling on its surface, or mirrored in the opal shimmer of its spume?

No, I tell you, nothing is lacking in the harmonious series of light effects which tint this world and its enchanting skies, not even antithesis, not even profound darkness—for, though it is true that dark nights are rare for the Starians, they nevertheless do come occasionally, when some lingering moon, or even some pale sun in its decline, appears alone, veiled by an atmosphere of heavy clouds.

Star, then, also has its shadows.

XX.

Oh, the brilliant and gentle night! A breath of warm wind brings us the roaring of the sea beating on the marble cliffs; then, at intervals, other, more distinct, sounds coming from the neighboring forests throw our souls—already amazed by such a beautiful spectacle—into an abyss of dreamy contemplation.

On the world of Star, melody comes from every side, almost as widespread as the air skimming over the ground and rustling in the grass. Not only has Nature given birth to multitudes of birds, almost all with musical voices, but even mammiferous animals are heard—their passionate cries being songs the traveler hears at a distance with delight.

If there are humans in this harmonious world, they must stop sometimes to listen to the chords produced by a sort of tree-gourd, swinging to and fro in the breeze. The fruit of this forest tree, called the *lartimor*, is suspended on long, flexible stalks, or peduncles, and consists of a nut with a shell of unusual hardness and elasticity. At maturity, the top of the nut turns toward the ground and opens, or, rather, uncovers itself and allows the liquid that fills it to run out. The empty shell remains thus for several years without alteration, and the sounds produced by groups of these shells of various diameters knocking against each other are harmonious notes which the wind makes sigh or roar according to whether it is calm or tempestuous.

Ah, yes, if there are humans on this world, the *lartimors* must have more than once revealed to them the harmonies of Nature.

XXI.

Let us leave our somnolent and contemplative reverie, for Ruliel is rising to chase the penumbra from the sky; the white sun appears, and soon our eyes, aided by its brilliance, have encompassed the final limits of the horizon to the east.

As the light delineates objects more distinctly, we experience vague thrills of hope and fear. Finally, we cannot doubt it: it is indeed the distant prospect of a great city that we see at the very extremity of the visible horizon. Quick! forward, oh! hurry—for we long to meet and question the prince of creation on this splendid planet.

XXII.

Despite being carried away by curiosity, we are stopped in our course by the disturbing scene of a combat taking place over our heads. A graceful bird of azure blue, with a beak and lineups of gold, appears before us. On its neck, it wears a white ribbon, a sign of domestication, and its presence also tells us of the proximity of habitations where the *citos*—which is the bird's name— is one of the creatures most prized by the peoples of these countries. Suddenly, two black, shaggy birds with elongated heads and dreadful red eyes spring upon the blue bird and, each seizing one wing, turn it upside down as if to tear it to pieces. At the cries of the *citos*, a white bird of monstrous size cleaves the air and, dealing two blows to the pirates with its enormous beak, rescues the *citos* and throws its dying attackers at our feet.

I have learned that the *citos* are revered and cherished birds, the agents of happiness, it is said, almost household gods for the Starians, who raise them in their houses, sometimes in flocks and sometimes singly. At just, this was for pleasure and, later, a little out of superstition. But the *citos* has a fierce natural enemy: the hideous black bird called the *zayou*, or bird of ill omen, which might quickly destroy the species, if the inhabitants of those countries did not, for its defense, take care to provide and instruct a kind of giant eagle to be the shepherd of each flock, and to rescue its charges when, by chance, as in this case, one of them wanders a little too far from the domestic roof and is attacked by the *zayous*.

XXIII.

What a land of extraordinary and variable aspects! At this moment, a dark, thick cloud comes to obscure Ruliel, the white sun; and, although it cannot completely obliterate the light of that great disc, which is still visible through a mass of gray mist like a bright moon on a clear night, nevertheless, it has darkened its penetrating radiance.

At other points in space, the red and blue suns, with rays crossing areas free of clouds, slightly change certain portions of the landscape, and color the mountains of the horizon an intense violet.

But the cloud passes across the face of Ruliel, and immediately, the tints of pale, colored light are obliterated.

XXIV.

When the winds drive along cloudy flocks, and only the colored suns are above the horizon, their rays escaping through the rifts in the misty fabric, it sometimes happen that a traveler may discern with his eyes little humps of blue, green, or rose puffs running and fleeing in the direction of the wind.

XXV.

Here, even animal nature might seem fantastic in its diversity. We have already encountered some very unusual animals in our path. But now, desirous to approach a new creature, a quadruped with close, white fur, much to our surprise, it seems to grow in size as it flees from us, so that after a certain number of paces, its volume has more than tripled. We accelerate our pace to take hold of this singular phenomenon; but, just as we are about to seize it, we see it rise into the air, first laboriously, then rapidly, without moving anything but its neck, which seems to serve it as a rudder. It disappears, carried off by a strong gust of wind, and goes to lower itself into a forest of orange-leaved *syphus*.[9]

---

[9] Here is what the Starian naturalists say of this animal, which they call the *psargino*: Its skin, which has great extensibility, is only attached at the eyes, the mouth, the other natural openings of the body and the soles of the feet. Over the rest of its expanse, it is only juxtaposed to another membrane, or internal skin, having the property at the animal's will of secreting a gas fifteen or twenty times lighter than air. The *psargino*, thus filled by gas, becomes a sort of balloon lighter than the atmosphere, and it makes use of this property to rise into the

XXVI.

The day is advancing, and we are about to stop at a bush with blue leaves to gather its perfumed, shining black flowers with distinctly moiréd petals, when we realize that our course has brought us to the entrance of a small market town, itself not far from the great city which we seek and which spreads out its immense suburbs in the distance. At this moment, our curiosity is about to be satisfied, our hopes and fears to find the humanity of this world, so different from ours, overwhelming and supernatural in strength, intelligence, and majesty, is about to be fulfilled.

We go forward; a small group of individuals of the Starian race appear. They are like us! These are truly the same mortals we know. Here, as everywhere, man is man; Nature, until now, has not produced anything more perfect.

XXVII.

To be sure, in structure, the human species on the planet called Star is like ourselves; but with regards to the forces of reason, spirit, and heart, we will have numerous occasions in which to compare them with us.

---

air and escape its enemies. A kind of aperture, furnished with valvules on its abdomen, relieves it of part or all of the gas burdening it and serves for descent to earth when the predator has lost its track. (*Note from the Author*)

XXVIII

Impatient to penetrate to the heart of this unknown world, we have established ourselves without delay in the midst of the powerful city which had appeared to us in the distance. With its buildings and wharves, it borders an iridescent sea and the mouth of a river which, at this point, comes to mix its placid waters with the agitated waves of a Starian ocean. The city's immense harbor is filled with vessels around which cavort *talersis*, huge aquatic beasts that the Starians have tamed for the service of ships plying the sea. We watch one of these ships arriving from the island of Infressia and entering the port in full sail, but still drawn by two *talersis*.

XXIX.

Viewed from a distance, the buildings seem of a bizarrely twisted architecture, but our attention is immediately and entirely drawn to the living section of the city. Indeed, as we go forward, it is impossible to turn our eyes from the masses of people who restlessly swarm over its docks or are engulfed in the streets of this great metropolis.

Approaching more closely, we see that these people seem to consist of two nations, two very distinct races who live together and scatter pell-mell in the maze of the city.

Before any further investigation, we note that the first race is comprised of beautiful, noble, and strong individuals—of both sexes. The second race is small, hairy and remarkable for their large, creased and drooping ears, adorned with silky hair, especially among individuals of the female sex. The first race is the closest to the human species: they are strong and intelligent; they are the superior and dominant race on Star.

The second race is an inferior race, or, to be more precise, a race of perfectible animals, endowed with more intelligence and ability than any of the others and, like human beings, gifted with effective hands and the faculty of expressing their ideas through the use of speech. These are the *Repleus*, the subjects of the Starians, who rule and command them and have reduced them to domestication.

The Starian race is without kinship to the species of the *Repleus*. The former is to the latter what the horse is to the donkey, and their coupling produces only half-breeds, incapable of further reproduction. According to their means and personal needs, the Starians possess one or several *Repleus*, raised and instructed in different functions, but especially for service particular to the household. The average height of a *Repleu* is a little over a meter; they walk upright, are agile and tough, and, in comparison to the Starians, their larger hands and feet have far more dexterity. Finally, their lives are half as long as those of the Starians.

XXX.

Horse-like beasts and vehicles streak through the streets; on the river and in the bay, boats and gondolas are drawn by *talersis*, cetaceans swimming at water level with incredible speed.

XXXI.

The Starian women are extremely remarkable, not only for their beauty, but even more for certain charms more particularly valued among the peoples of Star, that is to say, their nobility, propriety and integrity.

The men distinguish themselves especially for their strength, candor and activity: strong, frank, and active. So are the Starians.

XXXII.

Such is a Starian city at first glance: under a magical sky, amidst a superb and varied, expansive and lusty nature, it presents itself with its monuments mirrored in the tides of a translucent sea which, at once, reflects its palaces, its vessels and the multicolored fires of its suns.

XXXIII.

The Starian peoples are monogamous. The pure family ties, which are commonly found amongst them, illuminate their private lives with a gentle radiance of immaculate and permanent serenity. Does it not seem that, on such a magnificent planet, the needs of the heart, wild and intoxicated by Nature, must also be magnificently satisfied? Furthermore, there are no domestic servants among the Starians. These degrading services are left to the *Repleus*, almost all instructed to perform the lower functions of the household.

XXXIV.

Along with the *Repleus*, the *citos* is an indispensable fixture of a Starian house. These blue family birds, when in a flock watched over by a large, white bird, serve the Starians by ridding their houses of flies and other annoying insects. The *citos* is occupied part of the day in hunting insects; but, provided that it is prompted, it knows how to make a human habitation resound with low but sweet songs in which every variation is a complete melody.

The blue birds, with their beaks and wingtips of gold, reproduce with difficulty, but enjoy remarkable longevity. They are a part of the residence where they are raised and almost always die when transplanted to another place. A Starian house dispossessed of its family of *citos* will be considered cursed and will be deserted by its inhabitants. A *citos* isolated from its fellows and raised with a child, or long receiving the attention and caresses of its master, becomes his familiar for the rest of its life, and dies when the cherished person dies, or if a prolonged absence separates them. When a *citos* has bonded empathically with a Starian, it can then leave the domestic roof and travel with him; in addition, it knows, according to circumstances, how to comfort, console, or cheer its master with touching melodies, so that the person always finds the songs in harmony with the state of his soul. It is even claimed that the bird, having become empathic, can feel for another person loved by its master the same sentiments of goodwill and tenderness, and that it soon comes to echo harmoniously the passion of two lovers.

XXXV.

The Starians do not impose domesticity upon the half-breeds that result from the coupling of a Starian with a *Repleu*. Such individuals, begotten of improper relations, are today rarer. They are designated by the name of *Cétracites*. Almost all of them are born of female *Repleus*; a Starian woman who would forget herself to such an extent would be cursed and rejected by her people. The *Cétracites* cannot themselves have offspring; Nature has rendered them sterile. In general, they lead a miserable, and most often criminal, existence in the underworlds of populous cities.

We will have to return to this race, amongst whom several individuals became famous in the history of the Starian peoples.

XXXVI.

In walking through the city and its surroundings, the stranger, who sees on every side fountains of almost scalding hot springs, is astonished to discover conditions so well disposed to render human life easy and agreeable.

If we go back to the eastern suburbs of the city, our eyes are presented with splendid homes, surrounded by gardens where leaves and flowers assume an admirable brilliance. From orchard trees, in season, hang fruits which are bright, superb, savory in aroma and taste, with glazed, sweet and juicy flesh.

XXXVII.

Certain plants of these happy regions do not germinate or bear fruit until the arrival of spring and summer, when the light and heat of the suns have a quickening effect upon them.

Ruliel, the white sun, for the most part governs the climate, the seasons and the vegetation. In their changes, all large plants follow its annual ascending or descending progression along the ecliptic. Urrias, however, causes the ripening of certain garden plants bearing creamy fruit of an exquisite flavor. The fruit, which develops very quickly, promptly spoils. But the plant bears fruit several times a year, since a revolution of Urrias around Star is completed in less than sixty days.

The approach of Erragror, the blue sun, determines the maturity of other plants, useful to the arts and to industry. Finally, the heat of Altéther, the green sun, prompts, in the juices of some plants sensitive to its influence, the production of perfumes dear to the lovers of sensual pleasure. The emanation of these perfumes, voluptuously striking the sense of smell, have the property of throwing the soul into a drowsiness accompanied by the most delightful sensations and reveries of indescribable charm.

What more could one say of the Starians' gardens, if not that the constant union and progress of all these suns on the sky's plains cause to spring the most charming and varied flower-beds, overburdened with subtle fragrances from all their flowers, elegant in color, in pattern and in every graceful detail.

XXXVIII.

It is principally in the warm valleys and along the streams that the Starians know how to grow the largest and most beautiful *celsinores*, surely the largest corollas in a world so richly endowed. The *celsinores* are the gigantic flowers of a plant which meanders along the ground and covers it at some distance with branches adorned with finely serrated leaves. Its flowers, festooned with the most delicate colors, measure on the ground a length of more than two meters; they have the form and dimensions of a spacious cradle. By ancient usage, *celsinores* are consecrated to marriage, decorating the nuptial beds of young couples who, in the splendid sanctuary of love, customarily spend their wedding night on beds of velvety and perfumed stamens.

BOOK TWO

ANCIENT HISTORY

The Heroic Times

We have said enough to describe the general physiognomy of the new world we have discovered and to
picture the setting and conditions of humanity's existence upon it and under its skies. If some vague and incomplete shade still prevents the imagination from
clearly perceiving the features of this marvelous world,
the history of Starian society, which we are about to recount, will definitely give us a better comprehension of
the planet and dissolve the mist through which the mind
was forced to see it until now.

As always happens when men seek each other out
and assemble to live under a common law, to constitute
themselves into a society, heroic legends and traditions
most often remain the only documents by which the
historian may study those times which are called
mythological.

In the first centuries of the societies of Star, three
founding nations present themselves to us, each from a
far corner of the world, each possessing the rudiments of
civilization based upon mythological traditions. From
whence came these peoples, or rather, from whence
came Starian humanity? Did all the races of Star have a
common origin? Each of these three nations prided itself

on its antiquity. All three claimed to have been the cradle of the human species; none but their respective gods had created the first men. Yet, they were, as we said, each from far-flung regions of Star. From this, one might infer, in all logic, that the first humans were born no one knows where, were created by a God who was not one of the known gods, and that no monument or tradition had preserved the memory of that sublime effort of creative nature. Alas! how many doubts and worries would have been spared mankind if that God, after completing his task, had deigned to speak to his first creation! But no, the first men were not even conscious of the act of which they were the object; they did not even feel the touch of the mysterious hand that presided over the very making of their beings.

The three founding nations were the Savelces, the Tréliors and the Ponarbates, and their capital cities were named respectively Savel, Trélée and Ponarbas. The history of ancient Star is practically summed up in the history of these three peoples. We will now attempt to recount their major chronicles.

The Savelces

The dominion of the Savelces, which eventually embraced all the middle and southern parts of the eastern continent, was first confined to the territory held by Savel, a city located on the shores of the iridescent sea to the south of the continent.

Theocracy was the first form of government among the Savelces, so their history is intimately connected with the fables by means of which their priests had won the faith and veneration of the people during the primitive stage of their development. The Savelces' religious beliefs were remarkable for more than one reason; their mythology rested entirely on the following tale:

"In the beginning, on the earth and in the sky, there was Panéther, who later became ruler of the gods. But besides him, there also existed the Oxyure, a small, worm-like entity. Panéther, having only the Oxyure as a companion, mated with it and produced a beetle. Panéther, upon seeing that more perfect animal, united with the beetle, and the result of that union was a bat.

"Now, Panéther proudly began to contemplate his work, and it was from his union with the bat that were born the first man, named Poub, and the first woman, called Minelis.

"When Panéther saw the marvelous creature called woman, he wanted to fight with the man for her; but Poub had already made Minelis his mate and the two humans had several children.

"Nevertheless, Panéther, tormented by lust and passion, forced Minelis to mate with him; that the fruits of her infidelities were several gods, who presided over the things of nature, under the watchful eye and supreme dominion of Great Panéther

"These gods, Panéther's sons, were sterile, but mankind multiplied infinitely."

A cult and ceremonies were instituted at Savel and elsewhere in honor of these gods. The Bat, the Beetle, and even the Oxyure, had celebrated temples and numerous and contentious priests. Abusing the credulity of the people, they disputed with one another over matters of power and preeminence. Factions led by the priests of the Beetle on the one hand, and those of Rerriton, the god of fire on the other, became dogmatic enemies and bloodied the land for more than a century.

Meanwhile, travels and navigation, having become easier through the training of the *talersis*—which the Savelces were the first to domesticate—gave some rest to that unhappy people, so tormented at that time. Seafarers from Savel were the first to land on an island in the ocean surmounted by a peak now consecrated to Rerriton. This island was nothing more than an enormous volcanic mountain with a base plunging deep into the depths and a summit belching smoke six times as high as the highest mountains on Star. It rose above the ocean like a terrible beacon, which could be seen even from Savel.

In Starian antiquity, the Savelces were the most ignorant and the least wise of all the peoples, and those for whom history has the most to be ashamed about, for they were a warlike and fanatical race, a conquering nation.

The priests of Rerriton, having finally become the strongest power in the land, smashed the altars of the other gods, including those of Panéther himself, and imposed on their people the exclusive worship of their god.

The devout—and the hypocritical—amongst the Savelces had the custom of making pilgrimages to the mountain of Rerriton; those who climbed to the greatest height on the slopes of that immense mountain were venerated as saints and considered prophets of the god who had put into them, it was said, a spark of the purest fire. Some of those fanatics perished during their descents; others, attaining prodigious heights, found themselves seized by a dreadful vertigo and, half-asphyxiated by the rarefied atmosphere, were struck down by insanity. When they returned, their fellow Savelces did not fail to attribute their madness to divine inspiration. Then, they were dragged from market town to market town to instruct and fanaticize the people, who listened to their ramblings.

It was because of the preachings of one of these religious madmen that the first war between two nations of Star began, and that the power of the Savelces was extended over their peaceful neighbors. That man, named Stratiote, had been struck with insanity during an eruption of the mountain and had returned to Savel raving, preaching war and conquest. The priests and the majority of the nation deliberated at first; but Stratiote, having assembled the people on the shore, threatened them with the fury of Rerriton. The Savelces believed they saw the god's blazing mouth and heard his roaring in the sounds made by the volcano. Nothing more was necessary. The Savelces took arms, equipped themselves and, under the command of the inspired madman, they threw themselves upon their neighbors who, understanding nothing of such madness or cruelty, unknown until then, scarcely defended themselves, thinking instead to recover their independence when reason returned to their conquerors. This war and invasion lasted nearly six years, that is, as long as the eruption of the volcano. At the end of that time, the Savelces found themselves masters of an empire extending several thousand leagues.

Luckily, the nations conquered by the Savelces, after having consulted among themselves, had no trouble shaking off the yoke of that handful of raging fools. But, so that, in the future, no such scourge might fall again on them, they all sent delegates to Savel, where, united in an assembly, they founded a confederation which preserved the name of the Savelce Empire.

Such was the influence that the small tribe of Savelces had over the Starian civilization in the east and south of the eastern continent.

The rest of the history of this society, established

through the need to repudiate war and invasion, offers nothing worthy of reporting in this historical survey. The subsequent social life of these peoples is as peaceful as their beginning had been tormented.

The Ponarbates

At about the same time that religious convulsions were creating the Savelce Empire, the city of Ponarbas, located in the west of the western continent, began to arise out of obscurity. Originally, the Ponarbates were nothing more than the poor and ignorant clans of those regions, who, without religious or social dogmas, were gropingly organizing their half-savage communities. The country occupied by their tribe had a magnificent climate in which, without cultivation, the soil produced everything necessary to life. Material needs, always easily gratified, increased from that time because of the well-being already achieved. Gradually, the eagerness for physical pleasures among certain families gave rise to the desire to consult one another and to live, trade and work together. A certain number of families gathered and the city of Ponarbas was founded in a valley splendid with vegetation.

In the contract of union of those few hundred individuals, it was agreed that children, the aged and the disabled—without being separated from their families—would be supported by society, and that no one, for any reason, could own more land than he himself could cultivate; in a word, no one could own land of size and value impossible to manage or cultivate individually. It was held as a principle of honor and of law that one should only consume the fruits of one's labor and trade.

It is almost impossible to describe what a society thus established, consumed with activity and insatiable needs, was able to produce in riches and luxury. It was such an unprecedented spectacle and so encouraging an example that the Ponarbates' neighbors, the other hunting and pastoral tribes that lived nearby—all wise and gentle peoples—came closer together and eventually adopted the model of Ponarbate society, from which they borrowed laws and teachers.

The multiplication of these powerful laboring and consuming hives, banded together for work and commerce, carried the Ponarbate Empire to the highest degree of luxury and wealth.

Occupied with material things, accustomed to relying upon themselves, and further, confident in their own intellects and virtues, the Ponarbates imagined no gods. Their first moralists and philosophers attributed the original creation or generation of mankind to ancient transformations of animal species, that happened when some individuals, by chance, gave birth to superior types which formed a new stock. Thus, humanity, according to them, was descended from the *Repleus*, which themselves were descended, thousands of centuries before, from another kind of animal immediately inferior, and so on.

Indeed, without religion, the Ponarbates, finding in the splendor of their Heavens a source of infinite admiration, instituted a solemn cult for each of the principal stars; but these cults were simply the sincere and naive testimony of their admiration, for the Ponarbates never dreamed of worshiping them as gods. The notion of religious faith—praying, worshipping, fearing—was always absent from their minds. Besides, in that society, were not the many the Providence of the few? Thus, they had never known any other religion than their admiration and praise of the wonders of Nature and its dazzling sky.

The Ponarbates had the custom of depositing in their temples the most marvelous samples of their skills, turning them into veritable artistic and industrial museums on the pediments of which were engraved this formula that summed up their people's social compact: *Labor and Lavishness.*

The Ponarbates were the first to capture and tame the amiable blue bird with gold wingtips, the *citos*, that faithful guardian of the homes of Star, which bonds empathically and instinctively with its master and which always sings gentle songs to soothe his pains or magnify his pleasures. Such is the origin of the intimate attachment that the Starians have since felt for this bird with its graceful, elegant form and delicate, charming coloration.

If all the peoples of the western continent did not adopt the customs and social forms of the Ponarbates, they often visited them to observe the marvels of their industry and arts. Even the highlanders from the picturesque regions watered by the river Inrer were always flocking to Ponarbas, as if on a compulsory pilgrimage, and, tribe after tribe, left the tormented soil of their homeland to come and admire Ponarbas, its beautiful climate, its prodigious commercial activity and, after work, all the pleasures it offered in every material aspect.

The Tréliors

Amongst all the small cities which, at the barely discernible dawn of civilization, were located on the banks of the Saguir river, one would hardly have noticed the town of Trélée. Rising above its initial obscurity, it owed the ascendancy it later exercised over the destinies of Star's northern peoples to the basic notion of re-grouping under the same faith and the same flag innu-merable tribes which, up to that time, had crawled along in the abject barbarity of a life employed in satisfying gross appetites.

In fact, among all the peoples of those regions, the Tréliors were already renowned for their liveliness of character and sharpness of intelligence, and were even more esteemed for the nobility of their race. Together, these qualities could not fail to eventually bring forth among them a natural enthusiasm for elegance of mind and body; but, in the era of which we are speaking, even with such physical and intellectual inclinations, the Tré-liors were still uncultivated savages, like the peoples dispersed around them.

In the middle of their city of huts, they ordinarily celebrated their national festivals with a public feast, hideous orgies which brought all ages together pell-mell. But, one day, in the very heart of a feast, suddenly ap-peared a woman, as if she were intent to take part in the banquet; she was adorned with divine grace; she was of a beauty unknown to their eyes. Until then, they would never have dreamed of conceiving so perfect and daz-zling a woman. Beholding that apparition, the Tréliors abandoned their smoking meats and the wine jugs; they awoke from their drunkenness and loutishness. Respect-fully, they pressed about the young woman. She was a messenger, descended from the sky. Their admiration was soon translated into gifts. They gave her a palace as a residence. Then, with growing enthusiasm, the imagi-nations of the young men were set afire; their verve blazed on behalf of the beautiful Starilla—and poetry was born.

They were not content to stop there. A cult was instituted on behalf of the Princess of Beauty; her palace became a temple; and her servants, naturally, became priests. In short, from that day onward, the religion of the Tréliors had started and, through it, a fortunate and peaceful transformation was accomplished in their laws and customs.

Starilla, say the Trélior mythologists, had only passed through Trélée; but her memory and faith in her remained. That memory was alive, that faith ardent—for the discourses and songs of her apostles, the poets, thrilled half the barbaric world with descriptions of her wondrous charms. *Facta est lux!* for those astonished people, who then shedded the dirty clothes of barbarity and, for the first time, attempted to lead an intellectual life.

After the apostolate of Starilla, which impassioned and regenerated the surrounding nations, Trélée found itself the city of beauty, the city of the arts, the holy city, and, as such, the capital of the peoples united in the same worship.

The government of the Tréliors was in complete conformity with their customs and tastes. Every five years, the delegates of the federated peoples of their empire gathered in Trélée and chose as the Executor of the laws they agreed upon the most beautiful of all the young women who had come there to contend for that position of authority. The laws were accepted and obeyed by the Tréliors with respect and happiness, since they seemed to be the emanation and the desire of their beautiful sovereign.

An art entirely in harmony with the customs of the

Tréliors was born in the temples of Starilla. Its purpose was the beautification of humanity, and it consisted of procedures which could produce or complement human beauty. This art, in a word, was a kind of beauty culture.[10] The priests of Starilla cultivated this art from the earliest times and were the first beauticians and plastic surgeons of Star.

The Tréliors sought beauty in physical form as other peoples loved the luxuriousness of clothing. The art of beautification became such a general practice among them that almost everyone was graceful and good-looking and deformities of the body had become the rarest matters.

Star also owed to the Tréliors the subjugation and domestication of the *Repleus*. The *Repleus* had, until then, remained wild in the hearts of the jungles or in uncultivated wastelands, and fled from the Starians. They lived in family groups, feeding upon fish, game, and fruits. When humans began to domesticate them, attempting to educate them, it was observed that individuals of the same family had a certain language of a few words or a few sounds among themselves, and it was believed that this ability could be extended; thus, they were taught to speak the Starian language. Then, their new masters saw that the previously wild *Repleus* were becoming increasingly perfectible and docile because of their lessons. In short, the Starians, until then the only educated race on that world, had brought from the state of Nature, the state of bestiality, another race, also intelligent, though inferior, who then lived side by side with them, having, like their masters, its own customs and

---

[10] : See *Essai de Calliplastie* by Dr. Cid (Paris, 1846). (*Note from the Author*)

tastes, its social relations and aptitudes. Nevertheless, the Starians kept their distance from the *Repleus*; I would not compare their relationship to that of animal and man, but of slave and master.

The empire of the Tréliors, more moral than material, extended from east to west, up to the borders of the Savelce and Ponarbate empires. Those empires, founded earlier than that of the Tréliors, included peoples who remained faithful to their own customs and beliefs and over whom the movement that had originated in Trélée had had little effect.

We have now come to the period when relations between the three empires began. Commerce and navigation reached their greatest development. It was in this era that ships launched by the Tréliors discovered the island of Tastot which was soon explored by other navigators. It was there that the Starian nations discovered another kind of humanity different from them: the Nemsèdes, or Longevites.

The Nemsèdes, or Longevites

The Tréliors discovered about a hundred of these people, living in small groups scattered over the vast expanse of the island of Tastot. The Nemsèdes were about one third taller than the tallest of the Tréliors; their hair was deep blue, their eyes soft green, their bearings grave, and their physiognomies gentle and benevolent. They were all of the same sex, or rather had no sex.

These people, who all knew each another they had long lived together, had eventually divided into small groups composed of friends, united in the greatest intimacy. They claimed to be more than a thousand years old. None of them knew a father or mother. But they remembered being born nearly all together and at the same time in the heart of the forest near trees whose fruits, in falling, spilled out a milk which was their first food. They had further noted that, during their childhood, Nature was infinitely more powerful than it was then they first met the Tréliors. Then, the highest trees grew more than two hundred cubits per year. The sour lime of the soil, heated by lightning and subterranean fires, had given rise to a multitude of new animals, which had never been since seen on the earth, and which had disappeared suddenly, because they lacked some of the basic characteristics necessary to life or reproduction. From the remains of these animals and plants came yet more fantastic beings; life took on new, exuberant forms. Will-o'-the-wisps sparkled in all the cracks of that fermenting compost. Finally, little by little, those incomplete creations came to an end, and the world took on the aspect that it offered today.

Despite their prodigious age, the Nemsèdes were not conscious of having lost either their strength or their youth. Those among them who had died had been killed in accidents.

Those people, who were endowed with superior reason, who had lived and reflected so long, were soon regarded with the utmost respect and admiration by all Starians. A great number of them decided to leave the island of Tastot in order to bring to the other peoples the lessons of their experience and wisdom. Among other humans, almost all the Longevites, incapable of physical passions, became enamored of an art or a science. Each of them pursued his preferred science or art without pause through the centuries; their influence on the progress of Star was great, and would have been even greater had it not been for the evils which later decimated the planet's people.

Among the groups, or families, of Nemsèdes which the Tréliors discovered in the forests or in the mountains, were three Longevites who lived alone on a small island, in a lake surrounded on all sides by mountains, without communication with the rest of their race. These three friends, revered amongst their fellow Nemsèdes, were named Cosmaël, Séelevelt and Mundaltor.

It was noticed that, when following the other Starians onto the continents and establishing themselves in diverse countries, the Nemsèdes never left their own families. Few of those strange people remained on Tastot; some thirty families, including a total of three or four hundred individuals, dispersed into every corner of the world.

The three friends, Cosmaël, Séelevelt and Mundaltor, traveled over almost all of Star, observed and studied the knowledge accumulated by generations in the sciences, arts and letters. Cosmaël chose to study the physical and natural sciences; Mundaltor the fine arts; and Séelevelt devoted himself entirely to philosophy and literature. These three Nemsèdes, united in soul and feeling, communicating to each other every observation and thought, thus embraced the whole of Starian knowledge. They lived in this way for several centuries, occupying themselves without intermission with the beloved objects of their studies; attentive spectators of the progress of thought and custom in the Starian societies, they collected, centuries after centuries, the essence of the experience that each generation left as its heritage.

Accordingly, we could, with just these three

Longevites, recount the history of the varied disputes that eventually arose between the three empires which comprised the ancient Starian world. But, instead, we will pass over the political history of the next eight centuries because, despite some tribulations, it is more often than not the tale of a peaceful era, fruitful in well-being, that produced many splendid achievements and a great number of generous actions.

The Slow Plague

The three sovereign peoples of Star were vying with each other in the way of progress of spirit and intellectual well-being when, about fifteen hundred years after the founding of the Savelce, Trélior and Ponarbate empires, that world of pleasant climates, splendid skies and rich, beautiful nature began to be troubled. The land of Star, so accommodating and well disposed to generously feed and delightfully support a strong race of men, seemed to belch forth all sorts of ills against those who then lived on its surface, and to become an injurious and harsh mother to its children.

At first, there were subterranean tremors that ran from one pole to the other and left in their paths vast fissures in the ground. At the bottom of those chasms boiled lava which poured out a horrible mephitis into the atmosphere. That was the signal of the Ill Times, which the Starians have also named the *Evil Age*. The movements of the earth's crust shifted the seas; soon after, the ebb and flow of twenty successive floods caused innumerable men and animals to die.

When the earth finally stopped shaking, the soil seemed to have lost its growing powers. Natural processes behaved as if they were deprived of their most energetic leaven, those that purposefully drove the strongest and tallest organisms. The once-great trees began to be stunted and, instead, whatever was left of the life-force appear to concentrate on the lower plants and inferior animals. At the same time that the large animals and the most complex plants disappeared from the earth, the Starians saw the rebirth of ancient species of fossil animals and rudimentary plants that had long buried in the strata of the earth—the grave of primitive and antediluvian creatures. Creation was turning back on itself.

A famine lasting several years was the result of this impoverishment of the earth. The Starians, crying out under the scourge, succumbed to the degree that, in the twenty-fifth year of the Evil Age, their numbers had been reduced by a third.

The *Repleus*, already inferior in numbers to the Starians, had been decimated in the same proportion; several families of Nemsèdes had also perished as victims of various cataclysms.

For a time, the fury of the evils afflicting Star seemed to subside; the earth adorned itself with fruit and crops as before. People attempted to collect themselves and to heal the wounds that had been dealt to their civilizations. But there was already present among the races of Star the seeds of an evil a thousand times more atrocious than all those which had preceded it. It was from this time that dated the *slow plague*, which turned the planet into a living inferno.

Its beginnings were insidious: it struck a few individuals here and there, thus revealing a new sickness, an illness previously unknown. From the onset of the disease until shortly before death, which was inevitable, it was accompanied by extreme intestinal pains—steady, burning and throbbing. On the average, death did not occur for ten long, agonizing years. Women, children, sailors and the inhabitants of the sea coasts died most quickly.

For years, that disease brought forth shrieks from the unfortunates it tortured—and yet, did not kill. The slow plague destroyed the entire organism one fiber at a time, thinning the bones, until at last death came to deliver its victims from their endless suffering.

Some months before they died, the plague-stricken discovered that their intestinal pains were decreasing; they began to feel an agreeable tremor, a veritable impression of pleasure, in their heads. Soon, the pain diminished further and even ceased. Those individuals, who had already been transformed into a near-cadaverous state, suddenly rediscovered the sensation of pleasure, which gained in intensity and became amazingly strong and permanent. Well! That, for the sick, was the cruelest moment. The excess of sensual pleasure which convulsed a moribund body and which could not be controlled became, by its very presence, the most appalling torment that the victim had yet to suffer. The plague-stricken would die panting in the midst of transports of pleasure which were devouring the remains of their hideous skeletons. Oh! it was horrible, and one could scarcely comprehend that state, even by comparing it to that of someone dying from consumption who, during each moment of an agonizing year, also suffers from an irrepressible spasm of love which deeply penetrates him with the incessant titillation of the most bitter sensual pleasure.

The slow plague, which, in the first months, struck only a small number of victims, spread little by little and reached the great majority of the Starian species. There was neither city nor tribe that was not visited by the plague; on the highways, there were families from every part of the world who were leaving their countries, going in opposite directions, searching everywhere for a more healthful climate or a remedy for their suffering.

Some *Repleus* succumbed to attacks of the slow plague, but the disease weighed very lightly on that domestic species.

The displacement of the nations, all leaving their countries and driven back in their wanderings, demanding help from each other against an evil that was becoming ever more frequent and atrocious, caused an intermingling of the races to such an extent that all nations were dissolved and all societies became unrecognizable.

It was then that, in that afflicted world, appeared one of those men capable of dominating crowds with their charismatic personalities. His name was Farnozas. He was eloquent and persuasive and had already acquired some celebrity in science and medicine, especially in the country of the Savelces, where he was born.

The Suicide

The slow plague had already lasted forty years. Almost all the seamen, and women and children had been, or were becoming, victims of the epidemic. In each town, there were only a few able-bodied men left amidst populations whose agonies made them lament in vociferous blasphemies. The despair of the sick often drove them to madness or suicide.

Farnozas, during this time, roved the world. With irresistible ardor, he harangued the multitudes who pressed around him. He recommended that the Starians, dishabituated to superstition for several centuries, try singular practices of his invention. Everywhere, suffering gave birth to the most despicable fetishism. Monstrous idols were worshiped and implored with transports of passion.

Still, the scourge gained in intensity.

Farnozas again set out to travel throughout the world, preaching; but this time, he threw out an immense cry of despair to the masses. According to him, it was the end; the annihilation of mankind was going to be consummated; two thirds of the population had perished in sixty years, the rest would drag along for a while, then die alone and unmourned. Then, he proposed to those who listened to him—mostly disconsolate plague victims—a course of action suggested to him by his unflagging and most sincere mercy. It was necessary to rob the Great Fear of its last nourishment; it was necessary, immediately and in one stroke, to annihilate the remainder of mankind; for the sake of humanity, it was necessary to quickly destroy humankind. Long outcries of agreement answered him on every side. Soon, he found himself in the midst of an army of lunatics, preaching suicide to all, and often publicly giving example.

All the idols, not long ago objects of the most extravagant honors, were thrown into the sewers.

Farnozas' sectarians, seeing that a large number of individuals were rejecting the new doctrine, set about to murder their opponents everywhere. Their favorite weapon was a small bow of fine steel with prodigious elasticity which, after a slight effort, quickly shot a small, extremely sharp arrow. This instrument has remained the weapon of choice of murderers among the Starians became it kills silently and perhaps more surely than any other.

Most of the Longevites, appalled by that homicidal folly, wished to use their influence (because of their age and generosity) to oppose Farnozas' views; but the mob, envious at seeing that race escape the attacks of the slow plague, scorned their orations and even involved them in the project of destruction. Some of the most celebrated Nemsèdes were thus assassinated in the midst of their preaching. Arganture, Pérannor, Narraful and others less well-known perished in this way.

The three friends, Cosmaël, Séelevelt and Mundaltor, managed to get away from the Farnozians and resolved to try by all means to escape death and to preserve, if they could, some individuals, or reproductive types, of the Starian race.

An innumerable quantity of angry disciples, anointed by Farnozas, came and went in every direction, forcing people to commit suicide or delivering death to all who fled their mission. Many faint-hearted people preferred to kill themselves than to be killed; others feigned enthusiasm and were admitted among the drawers of the bow, hoping thus to buy time and, later, be able to escape their fate.

The following play, which I have translated, retaining as much as possible its original qualities, will present a picture of the cruelties of that mournful epoch in Starian history better than any description. It was written at the time of the last and most furious preachings of Farnozas.

MASSACRE DURING THE SLOW PLAGUE
(*A Savelce Poem*)

I. The Sick Mother

Pain alone replies to human prayer!
   Successively, I've implored all gods, from the Eternal
Intelligence to the idols of unclean animals, but my sick-
ness has become only more consuming.
Pain alone replies to human prayer!

Pain, more than the gods, reigns supreme.
   Oh! most certainly, a powerful and sympathetic God
would not leave each man, each fiber of his being
writhing for ten years under the dreadful lacerations of
this slow plague.
Pain, more than the gods, reigns supreme.

And my children's breath is soiled by the plague.
   All, save my eldest son, have succumbed to attacks of
the scourge. At this very moment, they turn over and
over, prey to its evil convulsions.
My poor children! Their breath reeks of the plague.

Mother, I'm burning; oh! come and soothe my pain!
   Last month, your father died, as dried as this iron bar,
suffering from acute voluptuousness, in the anguish of
the most agonizing pleasure.
Mother, I'm burning; oh! come and soothe my pain!

If I still had a heart, my pity would be vain.

For seven years, your mother's bowels have also burned with the fire that consumes you. Patience, children; you are young, without strength, and the sickness will be shorter for you.

If I still had a heart, my pity would be vain.

Listen, then, to the songs that rise from the plain!

Oh! if it were the sound of Farnozas' disciples, children! we would be saved and cured; for death would be near.

Now, do you hear those songs that rise from the plain?

II. Song of the Drawers of the Bow

Farnozas! A dread reinforcement is on its way!
We are two hundred thousand, and the immense corps
Is dedicated and arrayed for your work of slaughter.
Farnozas! A dread reinforcement is on its way!

Observe: all are writhing and torn in our retinue.
It's the plague; our ranks are all lost in misery,
Our sole war cry is: Oh, agony! Oh, agony!
Observe: all are writhing and torn in our retinue.

Only blood can soothe the gnawing pain.
For during the carnage and its fiery enthusiasm,
Our bowels no longer feel the oppressing cramp.
Only blood can soothe the gnawing pain.

Already, the human race bends before us.
Guide us, Farnozas, whose profound compassion
Will extirpate humanity from the world.

Hurrah! The human race bends before us.

We are blessed, we who worship death.
The vying crowds, bring us their heads
And everywhere, days of massacre are jubilees.
We are blessed, for the work we do!

III. The Plague Children

Have you lost the fragrance of youthful, untainted flesh?
   Has the habitual stench of corpses deadened your
senses, my fine bloodhounds? Alas! for so long the earth
has had no other perfumes. Come in! In this hut there are
still shreds of human meat throbbing and quivering.
Come, expel these remains of life. This way! This way!
Have you lost the fragrance of youthful, untainted flesh?

Kill these eleven children, withering in their beds.
   These children are mine. What! are you crying, poor
little creatures? Ah, forgive me for having conceived you
and having carried you in my womb; but thank me for
ending your suffering, since, in your agony, there can be
no rest but in death, and no hope but in annihilation.
Kill these eleven children, withering in their beds.

*Their death is quick! Soldier, how fast you dispatch
them!*
   Your blade has already driven into the throats of the
first eight. Stop a little! so I can embrace the three that
remain before they go to join their brothers. But, above
all, don't touch my twelfth child, my eldest son. You
must respect the one the plague spared.
   Stop, soldier! my turn is coming, and I also tremble!

Yet stop, soldier! How fast you dispatch us!

IV. The Charge of the Bowmen

THE MOTHER: Treachery! Treachery! They're taking away my healthy child; they're taking away my oldest son for the slaughter, too! Leave him, you barbarians! Stop, you monsters!

THE DECURION OF THE BOWMEN: *Form a circle. Soldiers, draw your arrows.*

THE MOTHER: But he's well, I tell you! You don't want to be crueler than the scourge… Cowards… But listen to me!

THE DECURION: *Soldiers, bend your bows. Forward. Fit your arrows.*

THE MOTHER: By the stars, mercy! Don't forget it was I who gave up eleven of my children, that I'm giving myself to your shafts. Ah! for pity! be satisfied with my sacrifice.

THE DECURION: *Raise your bows, archers! Fire your arrows.*

THE MOTHER: Horrible! the ten darts have converged in a sheaf at his heart. Not one of you is innocent of his death. Ah! you're clearly true soldiers—hired assassins, unknown to the world before Farnozas came. Away, senseless butchers and blessed be the plague that will avenge me on you!

THE DECURION: *It's my turn. Let me strike her with my arrows.*

THE MOTHER: I'm dying! but suffering no more… Oh! how death is sweet… Soldier, thank you… forgive me!

THE DECURION: *All are dead here. Soldiers, put away your arrows.*

The Suicide (continued)

The seas, the islands, the forests, all inaccessible retreats were visited carefully by the people bent upon the destruction of the Starian race.

Some fugitives had employed ingenious means in attempting to escape death; but none succeeded, except the one who is venerated today as the savior and father of the modern Starian race.

Ramzuel was his name; a stranger to the disturbances of the world, many years before, he had left the country of the Tréliors, his homeland, and had retired to the center of the island of Infressia in order to pursue, in the quiet of meditation, physical experiments on the gravitation of bodies, since he had caught a glimpse of the possibility of counterbalancing its action without destroying the force which aggregated molecules. His discovery, although complete, still had to be simplified for purposes of application, when Cosmaël and his two friends arrived there.

Cosmaël had been Ramzuel's teacher and inspirer. When he knew of his student's discovery, he conceived the project of using it for his preservation and that of the Starian race. Ramzuel, aided by the vast knowledge of the Nemsède, soon perceived the means of eluding the barbarity of the murderers.

After further research, they ended their efforts with the construction of two machines, which we will call by the name they were to have later: *abares*. These machines of vast dimensions were ovoid in shape and sheathed in a metallic plating pierced only at certain points by little windows covered with pieces of the same metal. It was that metallic sheathing completely enveloping the *abares* upon which was exercised the physical force forming the foundation of Ramzuel's discovery. This force suspended the effect of gravity for the bodies enveloped within it, and even imparted to the *abares* a tendency to work more or less in the opposite direction to planetary attraction.

Ramzuel fitted the first *abare* with a reservoir of oxygenated air,[11] provisioned it with everything necessary to life, and had the three Nemsèdes, Cosmaël, Séelevelt, and Mundaltor, and his family, composed of his four children, his wife Corrilis and her sister Essula, embark.

The second, somewhat smaller, *abare* was attached to the first by a metal cable. It had been filled with precious books and instruments through the care of the three Nemsèdes; it was to be sacrificed in case of danger to the first.

Cosmaël and Ramzuel had the opportunity to test their machines when Farnozas and his legions landed on the island of Infressia. They hovered in space at a height which rendered them invisible to the army of suiciders, and, for the first time outwitting the frenzy of the Farnozians, set themselves down on the glaciers of the land of Bazoumrée, near the south pole of Star.

Meanwhile, Farnozas had resolved to put an end to everything; after assuring himself that there remained only a small number of able-bodied men in the world, he chose and designated to everyone the place and hour of the great suicide.

---

[11] Eventually, instead of a reservoir of air, navigators furnished their *abares* with solid chemicals the combination of which could produce air, and each day they would prepare the provision of air for the vessel as they would prepare the provision of food. (*Note from the Author*)

That place was *Cape Abyss*, an immense promontory facing the northern ocean of the eastern continent, at the foot of which the sea broke and swirled in tumultuous waves, sweeping away and pulverizing objects caught in its currents.

From every part of the world, the disciples of Farnozas drove old men, women, children and the sick before them, directing them, as in a vast battle, toward the fatal promontory.

The hunt lasted three years more, and during that time, Farnozas, uncertain whether he would really bring death to the very last man, and constantly living in fear that someone might escape him, sought every means of assuring the complete annihilation of the species.

The ravages of the slow plague were little felt among the *Repleus*; nevertheless, the individuals of that cowardly race remained filled with terror at the suffering they saw among their masters. Farnozas suggested the thought, and tried to persuade them, that never would that frightful evil cease as long as there was a single Starian left in the world to feed the epidemic. He well knew that fear would make them cruel; and he further realized that, seeing themselves becoming the dominant species of Star, they would join his purposes and kill all those who might have otherwise escaped him.

He was not mistaken, for while he conducted the humans to the funeral spot, the *Repleus* in the rear murdered the unfortunates who succeeded in breaking through the lines of the army of future suicides. Not even the few Longevites who traveled alone escaped their homicidal daggers.

At last, the human masses found themselves assembled at Cape Abyss. Ramzuel, adjusting the centrifugal force of his machines, followed them and, from high in the sky, witnessed the preparations of the immense holocaust.

On the appointed day, Farnozas' sectarians, harangued for one last time by their leader, after having successively pronounced formidable curses against the earth, the sea, and the Heavens, pushed the old men, the women and the children into the abyss with fury, and, afterward, to the last man, hurled themselves from the height of the promontory's cliffs.

Ramzuel, overwhelmed with sorrow, soared up to the highest Heavens, seeking another world for Starian humanity, dispossessed of its birthplace!

INTERMISSION

THE DOMINION OF THE *REPLEUS*

At the time Farnozas was hunting the Starians who were recalcitrant toward suicide, it is said that he hesitated a moment, not knowing whether he should include the *Cétracites* in the great murder of humanity; but, reflecting that this race was incapable of reproducing, and would therefore soon become extinct on its own, he sought instead to make them his auxiliaries. To that effect, he organized regiments composed only of the half-breeds and made them the rear guard of his army, with the mission of killing the Starians who might otherwise succeed in breaking through the first lines.

Command of the *Cétracite* soldiers was given to one of them named Portamoüt, who had already distinguished himself for his courage and ferocity.

The universal suicide having been accomplished at Cape Abyss, Portamoüt, respected by his soldiers and already at the head of an imposing legion, far superior in strength and cleverness to the masses of *Repleus*, needed little effort to establish his power over the species which, from that moment, had become dominant on Star. By means of disciplined *Cétracites*, he trained troops of *Repleus* in the handling of arms; almost all of the *Repleus* were found to have a taste for military practices and discipline. Also, they were soon transformed into braggarts, haughty and vain, carrying weapons which, for the first time, made them formidable.

Portamoüt divided his new army into several de-
tachments, which he sent to search every corner of the
world to discover whether any Starians had escaped the
massacre. It was found, in fact, that, hiding on islands
previously uninhabited, in the heights of lofty mountains, a few families had been able to escape. The *Repleus* completed the work of Farnozas; and humanity
disappeared entirely from Star.

In destroying the Starians, Farnozas had respected
their work: cities, palaces, monuments, riches—all had
remained in existence. How was all this seized, divided
and shared by the *Repleus*? There was an inordinate
amount of greed and, more than once, blood flowed
around the spoils. The *Cétracites*, the strongest and best
disciplined, made themselves rich and powerful above
all. The combination of their blood with that of the
Starians distinguished them enough for themselves; but,
even though they despised the unclean species which
they now dominated, they decided to elevate their own
parents and other relatives by creating, from that exclusively *Repleu* stock, a nobility which, shortly thereafter,
was made hereditary. Moreover, since the morals of the
average *Repleu* were far from irreproachable, it was decided that inheritance among the nobility would be
transmitted through the females, because it would then
be certain that the children born of them would be of at
least half-noble blood. Nobility had been unknown to
Star. The stupid and vain idea of establishing such dis-
tinctions had never sprung up in anyone's head before.
But, quite naturally, it was bound to appeal to the pride
of a *Repleu*. Moreover, from top to bottom, there were
none among them but rascals and villains; and there was
not a filthy and vile *Repleu* who did not regard with the

height of disdain another individual of his race yet more abject than he.

The Starians, having domesticated the *Repleus*, had found in them servants of passive submission and often cunning baseness. Yet, if they might complain of the gluttonous, cowardly and licentious character of the second order of creation, they consoled themselves in seeing that the *Repleus* possessed the intellect and taste for servitude. Despite the quarrelsome spirit the *Repleus* showed among themselves, there had never been any revolt or insubordination to fear; for the very foundation of *Repleu* character was a pugnacious and boastful cowardice, which only success or fear could render savage. When the Starian race was destroyed and had vanished from the surface of the world, the *Repleus*, with their quarrelsome disposition, brought to their mutual relations an almost bellicose spirit, preserving, however, the instincts of obedience and servility. These faults made them a species well fitted to a military state and discipline; likewise, in contrast to the Starians, among whom the army was nothing, for the *Repleus*, the army was everything.

Therefore, Portamoüt had little to do to draft the bolder of the *Repleus* into his armies, all the more so since he conferred money, power and honors on them.

The new nobility declared themselves fit only for the profession of arms.

Closer to human reason than the ignorant masses of the *Repleus*, Portamoüt, who wanted to be a lawgiver, did not consider his power strong enough, even with a savage and brutally obedient army; he also wanted to oppress the people with the tyranny of religious superstition. His father, a poor miner from the country of the Savelces, had been one of the last worshippers of the

Oxyure. He had raised Portamoüt in that religion and the latter, accustomed to the dogmas and ceremonies of the cult, did not seek the trouble of learning a new religion. Temples and altars were already in existence, dedicated to, according to the country, Ruliel, Starilla or Panéther. The *Repleus*, now transformed into priests of the Oxyure took possession of them and there unfolded a series of hideous liturgical masquerades. It is even reported that these new priests assembled a council in which the *Repleus* acknowledged themselves henceforth to have immortal souls and claimed a future paradise of pleasures, naturally reserved chiefly for warriors and members of the new clergy.

It is said that Portamoüt, seeing the prideful, yet base, instincts of the species he now governed, and comparing it to the majesty and sincerity of the Starian race, repented before he died of having been one of the instruments of the destruction of humanity on Star. He regretted, it is said, that that admirable world, that splendid Nature, had only for spectators beings who were degraded and incapable of feeling its charms and poetry.

Portamoüt married a *Repleu* named Oussanru. Since he could not have children, it was his half-brother on his mother's side, the *Repleu* Cassupif, who succeeded him. Cassupif married the empress Oussanru, by whom he had several children. Cassupif was an idiotic and feeble leader. The army chiefs and nobles, seeing the mental deficiency of their new emperor, were tempted to seize power and heaped up massacres upon conflagrations, and pillage upon rape. The empress Oussanru, having succeeded in assembling a certain number of loyal troops, sent as a gift to the rebel armies—as if she wanted to appease them—a considerable quantity of brandy and other strong drinks. The soldiers foolishly steeped themselves in the alcohol. For some days, there was nothing in the camps but orgy, drunkenness and brutalization. Meanwhile, Oussanru, knowing that her opponents were drunk and incapable of fighting, had her small, faithful band march against those inert masses. There was dreadful butchery and peace was reestablished.

Already the great majority of the *Cétracites* had died and, as a generation of *Repleus* had passed away since the Starians' suicide, those beings, of greater stature and intelligence than the *Repleus*, were now being venerated and regarded with superstitious dread. Soon, the astonishment which the old *Cétracites* inspired in the people gave way to a sort of cult. They were of a superior nature; the *Repleus* quickly made them demigods. The last to survive was the *Cétracite* Corlaop. He was actually deified and had temples while he lived—more or less like the Oxyure. It is further believed that the deceit of the *Repleu* priests strongly contributed to bringing about that result. Here, in a few words, is the history of the god Corlaop:

That *Cétracite*, who had attained an advanced age, after having successively outlived several females, married at the age of eighty a *Repleu* named Rédidou. At the end of one year, she brought into the world a child of *Repleu* blood. Corlaop, who could not remember that any *Cétracite* ever had an offspring, wanted to kill the *Repleu* woman and her son, when the high priest of the Oxyure, who was a relative and probably Rédidou's lover, interpreted the event as a divine miracle. Corlaop consoled himself for his misadventure by becoming a god in a splendid temple once consecrated to Ruliel.

Inheritance being transmitted through the female line, Cassupif was succeeded by his sister's son, named Bénoraou. That *Repleu* lord was certainly the most capricious and whimsical emperor of his species. Having heard that the Starians had once been stronger and more beautiful than the *Repleus* because they had flat ears and white, smooth skin, he wanted all his subjects to have their ears shortened and the hair removed from their skin. This was the occasion of much pain and gnashing of teeth among the *Repleus*; but Bénoraou insisted, and the *Repleus* soon went without ears and without hair; from being ugly, as they were, they became shockingly hideous. In the end, Bénoraou could not help recognizing this. Then, he directed everyone, on pain of death, to dye themselves scarlet from head to foot, and he himself led the way. This metamorphosis rather pleased the *Repleus*; their population, thus rutilant, became unrecognizable—the disguise favored pillage and debauchery. Soon, dissatisfied with the color red, Bénoraou had his people dyed successively blue, green, and so on, making his docile nation change, from one moment to another, from white to black.

His successor, named Corrip, was a great believer in etiquette; he preserved the custom of having his subjects dyed, but he assigned a color and a shade to each class and rank. He had reserved white for himself, his family and the high nobility. Then, all classes aligned themselves by colors and shades; at the bottom were the plebes who, for their distinctive color, were assigned light gray. Unfortunately, it was always happening that the gluttonous and dirty habits of the high dignitaries quickly sullied the whiteness of their bodies; this, with the filthiness of their dress, caused them to be confused with the *Repleus* besmeared with gray at the bottom of the social ladder.

While the emperor Corrip was spending his time debating the forms and usages of courtly etiquette with his ministers, his empire was being dismembered; several army commanders established independent kingdoms for themselves. After Corrip, we saw the lands of Star being divided into smaller states or kingdoms of the *Repleus*—always plundering and attacking one another, conquering each other in turn—just as their minds were steadily becoming more brutal and savage.

The factors that prevailed in the internecine wars of the *Repleus*, as well as in their domestic differences, were the chaos and evil spread by widespread panics. which happened frequently in connection with any absurd rumor, and which caused entire armies to flee, whether victorious or vanquished, or else which, in the twinkling of an eye and without motive, set individuals of the same nation to quarrel with each other and murder one another out of fear. Under these circumstances, every unhinged and fearful *Repleu* would mercilessly slay another *Repleu* that fell into his hands. At every moment, the soldiers of one army, or the inhabitants of the same city, seized by some ridiculous fear, would come to blows and exterminate each other with frenzy, up to the moment when, fear having become at last more intense than madness, all would begin to flee in every direction. These ferocious fears were explained, in part, by the extreme cowardice that is at the core of the *Repleu* character. Every government tried to legislate against these panics, without succeeding in controlling their excesses. In every country of the world, a person, whoever he might be, convicted of having shared his terrors with his neighbor was condemned to immediate execution at the stake. That law, which forced the *Repleus* to disguise their cowardice, contributed mightily to their exaggerating their boastful and bullying tendencies, which they have retained to this day.

Among the five or six kingdoms that then divided the inhabited lands of Star, the most important was that of Polymanie, for the reason that its people were permitted the most extravagances. We will hastily recount the principal events of its history, because familiarity with them will help achieve a clearer understanding of other events which followed later.

After a period of political tumult, during which certain *Repleus*, who showed themselves to be almost human, tried to establish a free, independent government, despotism and war returned, bringing in their wake a pugnacious mob of vain and bloody characters, whom the *Repleus* called heroes and always acclaimed, probably because they were the butchers of their stupid race.

The state of Polymanie had to suffer further misery, anguish and desolation in exchange for the glory which the martial leaders of their senseless, bewildered hordes always sought for themselves. Among the *Repleu* lords who successively occupied the throne of Polymanie were Coscolo, Rontalouf and Tortipu. They were the most celebrated among the kings of nations for the reason that they had had more *Repleus* killed than any other conquering despot, and because they committed perhaps the greatest crime of *lèse-Repleusité* that had even been perpetrated since the beginning of that race's domination.

The Polymanians made war on all their neighbors at once—on the Ursusottins, on the Gibbogrimes, etc. These, on their part, in waging war on the Polymanians, did not fight each other less, and it even happened that the *Repleus* of one nation would fight among themselves as well as with all other nations at the same time. Yet the *Repleus* were lazy and cowardly; but perhaps the apparent contradiction is sufficiently explained if one realizes that disciplined cowards were servilely obeying the orders of vain cowards.

Surely, the *Repleu* species would have had to multiply beyond measure to replace the waste of *Repleu* flesh being made by their so-called heroes, who never questioned what was the cost in lives of their follies. What was singular was that the more Coscolo, Rontalouf, Tortipu and others had their own armies slaughtered, the more those whom they had exposed, and whom they were going to expose, to death were fascinated and brutalized by discipline to admire their bloodthirsty extravagances.

After a period of more than half a century, a veritable orgy of blood, wars and political chaos, the *Repleu* world, depopulated, disgusted and exhausted, rather than surfeited and chastened, found itself enjoying an approximate peace.

At that time, a *Repleu* named Pansouillu was king of Polymanie. Pansouillu, not wanting to make war, ate a great deal, slept well and did not want to do anything else.

Then, after him, came other kings who themselves wanted to do something; but what could the mind of a *Repleu* king want, if not to vex and torture his nation a little? Some of those princes employed all the energy of their subjects in building mausoleums; and this is mentioned to show the extent of their pride.

When the *Repleus* were not making war upon others, they were sure to be fighting among themselves. Now, during the reign of one of the last Polymanian kings, named Cafon, a schism occurred among the priests of the great Oxyure, some of whom wanted to locate their paradise of future pleasures in the sky, while others wanted to locate it underground. Cafon himself had a pride truly worthy of a *Repleu*: that it was not too much for a king like himself to enter paradise body and soul. That was why, having at first embraced the belief of those who located paradise in space, he had his people build a tower whose pinnacle could touch the sky, so that, after his death, his tomb could be perched up there. Later, however, having been brought over to the doctrine of the priests who maintained that the happy abode of the great Oxyure was underground, Cafon had the tower torn down and excavated in its place a shaft of incalculable depth, destined to engulf his mortal remains.

Moreover, the Polymanians, despite their stupidities, inspired the admiration of the Ursusottins, the Gibbogrimes and other peoples; these did everything they could to resemble the Polymanians and all demonstrated in their behavior an almost equal insanity.

Later, we shall learn what event eventually overthrew in an instant the political and social structures of those varied kingdoms.

BOOK THREE

THE SATELLITES

Chapter 1: Tassul

I.

A strong, ascensional and slow stream
Took Ramzuel toward the sky's abysm.

II.

Once extricated from the vapors of the atmosphere, the *abares* which carried the last of the Nemsèdes and the only survivors of the Starian race in their ascension, took on a previously unknown speed.

Ramzuel's craft rose and rose, withdrawing with the speed of an arrow pointed toward the zenith.

Soon, they reached regions distant enough from Star that the planet, with an already phosphorescent aspect, appeared to the ethereal travelers to embrace the lower part of the sky.

Still they rose, and the phosphorescence became a true lunar light; they rose, and the world in its part of the sky was nothing more than an immense disc which startled the eye with its enormous mass.

They withdrew farther; but, at last, full of uncertainty and great distress, they stopped for a time in space.

At that very moment, looking around them, Ramzuel and the Nemsèdes were struck with terror by the dismal silence of the Heavens and the incommensurable solitude, full of light and emptiness.

Toward what place would they steer?

In the bosom of what world would they shelter?

The stars were still so remote…

It was then that the fresh and smiling face of Tassul came into view.

After a moment's reflection, they decided to direct their course toward that satellite, which is closest to Star in space.

Despite the infinite force of progression the *abares* possessed, they went astray for a long time in their pursuit of Tassul, which sped before them in its rotation around Star.

Discouraged, Ramzuel then stopped, daring neither to return to his original course, nor to advance farther in the seas of the void. By means of a special maneuver, which balanced the *abares'* centrifugal and centripetal forces, he had them maintain, at that point in space, a true and absolute immobility.

The Starians, despondent and anxious, looked around them at the scattered discs in the sky, craving and coveting a world, a land—less than that, the wreck of a planet or an asteroid where they could rest for a while.

III.

Rushing forward come a thousand clustered suns;
Turning stars fall away in their revolutions;

And all, rapid and fierce,
Surprisedly contemplate with their very eyes
Ramzuel immobile, hanging in space
And letting the entire universe pass;
Only the Starian *abare* stops like an atom
In the heavenly firmament, seized by the vacuum.

IV.

The human race dethroned from the planet Star
Believed they were condemned to die in the ether.
Silence and solitude… and nothing there
But the incommensurable and infinite sphere!
In undulations of cold light, the last
Of the Starians, for their place of final rest
Would have the empyrean, void and eternal.
Humankind would end there!
                      Yet Ramzuel
Perceived, rising from their horizon's lower sill,
A shimmering moon.
                        O success! intoxication!
The planet advanced, coming in their direction. . . .
Soon, as reason called upon calculation,
In that redeeming world they knew the Tassulian
Orb, which, for them, ended its circular path
And came to offer its hospitable earth.

V.

Indeed, that satellite after which they had run had
an impossible speed; but, having achieved its revolution
around Star, it returned to overtake the Starians at the

point in space where they had stopped, despairing of ever reaching it. Ramzuel guided the *abares* into the orbit which Tassul was to follow, and he soon found himself at the extreme limits of the atmosphere of that welcome world.

Once within the atmosphere surrounding the satellite, he maneuvered so as to travel for some time over its surface, and chose to disembark on an isolated location.

It was on the summit of a mountain that the Starians eventually landed.

At last, they had found another homeland: but alas! their hearts, gladdened by hope, immediately shrank as they let their eyes wander over those strange lands. At the surface of the ground, the physiognomy of Tassul had its own beauty, but it looked quite different from the world where they had been born; the things they beheld were not the objects that their eyes had been accustomed to see; they were indeed exiled to a new world.

In descending from the mountain where they had effected their landing, they found plains where the vegetation, compared to that of Star, seemed somewhat stunted. The color of the fields and of the woods covered with leaves was rather uniformly white, or a shade off from white to gray, as if, in a Starian landscape, the countryside had been covered with frost. Nevertheless, over that white and ash-colored landscape, brightly colored fruits and flowers gleamed as red, yellow and blue sparkles.

But what struck the Starians with surprise and admiration was the multitude of birds displaying colors similar to those of the flowers; in scattered and innumerable flocks, they appeared hanging in clusters amidst the white foliage, or flying about pell-mell among the flowers and fruits. The singing, multicolored bands gave the most fantastic animation to the plains of that world, where one could not take a step without seeing spring up pretty golden, violet, red and green birds like thousands of sparks flashing through the sky or agitating the foliage, all the while sending forth harmonious songs.

If the number of birds seemed prodigious to the Starians, that of other animals seemed considerably diminished; for they saw only a few rare beasts here and there.

After a first glance of inspection at this hospitable world, the Starians instinctively lifted their eyes toward their home planet, the object of all their regrets and love. At that moment, and from the place they stood, the horizon of Tassul, the first satellite of Star, was partly filled by the great planet which, like an enormous moon, covered a considerable area.

VI.

Then, its immense, pale globe over them
Extended in the sky its potent corona
And there set a scintillating pattern
  For its vast cupola.
All the fires of the suns scattered in the sky,
Reflecting on that disc, tracking their prints
  In a capricious way,
There caused to be mirrored shadows, rays, and tints.
At the magnificence of that orb of radiance,
With the warmest reflections and the colors of Iris,
The eye might have thought it saw the artist's palette
Of the angel who, landscapist of the heavenly vault,
  Painted the infinite worlds
  On the frescoes of paradise.

VII.

Besides the three Nemsèdes, the Starian family was composed, as we said, of Ramzuel, his four children, his wife, Corrilis, and her sister, Essula.

This group of travelers, after having parked the *abares* in a safe place, advanced cautiously in search of some trace of life on Tassul. Their search did not last long; for, after some hours of walking, they discovered, in the distance, a city located on the shores of a lake.

They approached it, trembling with uneasiness.

The first Tassulians who saw the Starians were extraordinarily surprised at the strangeness of their appearance and had all the people gather around them.

Ramzuel and Mundaltor, by means of an expressive and suppliant pantomime, told the story of their misfortunes, as they pointed to the cradle of their birth hanging in the sky. The differences in physical appearance which distinguished them from the people of Tassul made their adventures easy to believe. Kind and hospitable, the Tassulians helped them at once and, later, gave them lands on a fertile, though virtually uninhabited, continent. That continent was located on the side of the globe which perpetually faced Star as it seemed to orbit around Tassul. It was there that Ramzuel established his family, with the hope of beginning the regeneration of the Starian race.

Essula, Corrilis' sister, had been destined to live in celibacy; but Séelevelt the Nemsède had helped Ramzuel's wife understand the loss that the celibacy of her sister would cause her family, which needed to produce children in order to recreate the Starian race. Corrilis herself then went to Ramzuel and asked him to take

Essula as his second wife.

That was why the number of Ramzuel's children became very large.

VIII.

Let us now speak of the natives of Tassul, with whom the Starians came to live.

Ramzuel and the Longevites, ignorant of the language and customs of the Tassulians, believed for a while that their women were carefully guarded inside their houses, or that custom made it a rule for them not to show themselves in public. Their surprise was great, therefore, when they discovered that the individuals with whom they maintained relations had no wives, but that they themselves comprised the two sexes; in a word, that they were hermaphrodites.

The Tassulians, endowed with both sets of procreative organs, did not require a union with another individual of their species; they were able to beget and to give birth alone and by their own faculties.

Their dress was uniformly a sort of toga amply draped over their shoulders. The Tassulians, for the most part, were robust and tall, did not know luxury and practiced the most absolute social equality.

If the love of the sexes was something unknown and impossible on Tassul, it is said that they nevertheless found within themselves very ardent sources of natural happiness. Who can truly comprehend the joys of a solitary love, a love of self, a love always faithful, without jealousy, without regrets? The most absolute sentiment, the most constant passion, of Tassulian character was incontestably the passion of parenthood. Parental love was the life and joy of that race. How could it be otherwise? Free from the cares of conjugal love, all the desires of their hearts were poured out upon their children. Never, as among human males, did a gnawing doubt come to trouble their parental quietude. Besides, their children were engendered from their blood; each child was of the flesh of one alone; each was maintained in one's bowels and never was carried and nursed by a wife, indifferent or hateful. Among a race with two sexes, a child belonged to the mother and was connected to its father only by a very fragile bond, which sometimes broke in his eyes, as in the eyes of the world. How many fathers, having a profound and necessary desire for paternity, have regretted to not be more complete participants in the act of procreation of an individual of their blood?

Great, very great was the solicitude of the Tassulian for his children, and that solicitude was only equaled by the respect and affection of the children for the unique author of their days. The family, based on parental love and filial devotion, was strongly established among the Tassulians. Since marriage could not exist, children never left their parent to follow a stranger, and the progenitor eventually died, surrounded by his offspring whose loving thoughts followed him even beyond the grave.

In that society, woe to the sterile, condemned to live a life of solitude without hope of ever satisfying their need for love. Thus, almost all the Tassulians to whom nature had refused the gift of parenthood, resorted to early suicide. A peculiarity of the physical structure of that race furnished them with an extremely easy means of doing so. The heart of a Tassulian was under the influence of the will, and a vigorous effort of that will could stop the heartbeat: the will to die sufficed to kill.

The numerous species of birds found on Tassul were almost all endowed with two sexes. The mammalian animals, for the most part hermaphrodites, were only found in small numbers. The most common animal on that world was a kind of reptile called a *ball*, which, as its name indicates, has the form of a ball of white and livid flesh, without the appearance of members or external appendages. This reptile, which lives on dry grass and which walks, or rather rolls itself, along the ground by means of muscular contractions in its hide, long prompted the disgust of the Starians, who could not without dread look upon its fleshy mass, as big as a man's head, with its mouth slit surmounted by two holes at the bottom of which burned two always fixed eyes, without movement and without eyelids.

IX.

In the fine and frosted grass which carpets those fields,
  Gathers the tribe of the sons of Ramzuel.
  The father is with them: he is bent, being aged,
  And, trembling, he leans on the arm of Cosmaël.
  The children are arrayed around the *abare*
  Which once had saved their parents from extinction.
  Ramzuel prepares himself for death, which is near;
  All have received his kiss of paternal affection.
  He mounts the *abare*, there again taking his place,
  And he pronounces these phrases solemnly:
  "I wished the *abare* in which I have conquered space
  "Be my last shelter, my tomb in the boundless sky;
  "But before he vanishes into the void,
  "Your father gives to all here the immortal edict:

"Human beings, remember well my last words;
"May always and everywhere this sacred precept
"From father to son be repeated through the ages,
"The great rule, the eternal testament
"Given his children by the first of sages:

X.

"RESPECT MY BLOOD!"

XI.

All were still listening, when Ramzuel already
Was furrowing the fields of the infinite:
The Starians' eyes wished to fix his route;
But the *abare* rolled at random ascensionally…
The last seeing it in the hazy atmosphere
Through blue ether soaring into the depths of the air,
Sailed the *abare*, wandering in the sky,
At last, went to lose itself in Ruliel's eye.

XII.

At Ramzuel's death, his children and grandchildren
and great-grandchildren already numbered in the hundreds. Arts and letters had been preserved in flourishing
state, thanks to the three Nemsèdes, who, guardians of
all knowledge, had been the teachers of Ramzuel's children and had distributed the professions according to
individual aptitudes.

Under a fraternal government, the Starians lived for

a period of four centuries, multiplying to such an extent that their number soon exceeded that of the native race of Tassul. Although vaguely troubled by the tradition of their lost world, the Starians became accustomed to regarding Tassul as the red and inalienable homeland of their species, even with its dwarfed vegetation and its grayish life-forms, scarcely enlivened by its multitudes of precious birds. They considered as the only view the one they beheld—the view of a sky forever occupied by an immense planet, which reflected a phantasmagorical but pale and lusterless light.

Some more years passed; but, at the end of that time, it became obvious that the Tassulians and the Starians, having spread over every corner of that world, were going to suffocate on a world too small and incapable of nourishing their whole population.

On the part of the Starians, a council of those elected by the people was convoked: there, Cosmaël, Séelevelt and Mundaltor calmed the Starians' desperate anguish by showing them large-model *abares* which they had just had finished constructing; the Nemsèdes promised them, instead of Star, where they did not dare to venture, another world where the surplus population could emigrate. Therefore, it was decided that a flotilla of *abares*, under the command of Cosmaël, would, at an opportune moment, travel to Lessur, the satellite of Star located immediately beyond Tassul.

After a crossing, during which several *abares* were forced to fall back toward Tassul, three *abares*, each commanded by one of the Longevites, landed one hundred and fifty Starians on Lessur.

Before entering upon a description of that satellite, let us say at once that the first exploration of that world, twice the size of Tassul, sufficed to decide the Starians to establish settlements there, and that, on the advice they had been given, several hundred Starian families went there successively.

Chapter 2: Lessur

I.

When the ethereal navigators, guided by Cosmaël, arrived on Lessur, their astonishment was at its height. They left the ether's void, with its depths of transparent black, and began to float in the atmosphere enveloping Lessur. They hastened to let into the *abares*' interiors that new, pure air in order to breathe with full lungs. Immediately, their sense of smell was delightfully affected by a wonderful, mellow fragrance. They came to earth enraptured and only became accustomed to those scents little by little in order to more voluptuously inhale the nuances, different according to the breezes moving the waves of perfumed air.

On Lessur, the north and west winds have different fragrances; but nothing equals the sensations of sweet bliss sometimes sent by the enchanting and caressing perfumes of the breezes of evening or of the incomplete twilight of those lands. Those breezes almost always provoke a placid intoxication and invite sleep full of delightful quietude.

That fragrant atmosphere, that air covering the surface of Lessur, instead of coloring the sky blue as on Star or Tassul, tints its transparent depths a golden yellow, and its limpidity is only rarely tainted by clouds of silvery white.

Imagine, under that redolent sky, a land perpetually adorned with verdure, with vegetation often bluish, but also, more often, hidden under innumerable fragrant flowers, all of brilliant colors, exhaling perfumes of differing essences. These flowers, small in the grass, are enormously large in the trees. If Tassul was the planet of birds, Lessur, in the Starians' eyes, was that of flowers, and, above all, the enchanting land of soft perfumes.

In crossing the golden sky, the suns have a warmer and more intense brightness. Star, farther from this satellite, no longer overhangs half the sky with its circular mass, as on Tassul; but its still mighty disc sternly recalled to the Starians the traditional memories of their homeland.

Let us advance amidst this verdure and these flowers lit by this golden sky and breathe the air, varied slightly with perfumes according to the wind's direction. Let us go forward, for we want to meet the satellite's native race, and we are beginning to catch sight of the Lessurian people seated in the country's flowery shade.

II.

All grace and fire, the people of Lessur
Appeared to the Starians as emblems most pure
Of form expressing the life of the intellect,
Of sprightly and thinking flesh moved by spirit.
Life and thought, in that magnificent land,
On each, growing handsomer, carved the traits of a god.
An angelic race, all but immaterial!
Their pale, rose forms are expressive and beautiful:
Like a sunbeam, their coloring throws out a splash
Of mellow light infusing their rosy flesh;

Their clear, vermilion blood flows vibrating
Under the skin, rushing and sparkling.
But, especially, there brightly shone in each eye
A spiritual flame such that it could defy
A Starian gaze to stare into its power.

Our amazed travelers remained at a distance there.
They approached… Already those splendid folk
Had seen the Starians, and, advancing, spoke…
From their lips came a sympathetic harmony,
A language in which verse and melody
At every moment inspired improvised songs,
Translating all thought into harmonized poems.
In public discourse each clear and vibrant voice
Did not desire to use inelegant prose,
Only reserved for children, although in private
Spoken verse they scarcely would accept.
An admirable symbol of that artistic race,
It is the orator who bestows on his phrase
The large and prompt talent of a great composer,
The spirit of a poet and voice of a singer-
Who, in a rhythmic chant, with the subject's nuance,
Improvised both melody and cadence.

The Starians listened, moved by their recitals,
And followed, thrilled, those proud and gentle mortals,
Curious to sound their extra-human customs.

In the heart of a prairie, where pure fountains
Diffused the mildest freshness all around them,
A grove of green trees suspended a vault of blooms.
Beneath them, the earth, like a carpet, was adorned.
In daylight, among shaped flowers under that arcade,
A multitude of women would sing and dance.

Lessurian souls, those alabaster sylphs,
Whose flesh might have been formed of softened pearls,
Were seen to rise on sure and vigorous limbs,
Floating fragile, suspending themselves. As they were
Wafting thus, their voices sent through the air
Songs going to the heart, whose modulation
In gentle thrills conveyed an intoxication.

III.

The Starians were extremely delighted. Conducted to the hearts of their cities, they then began to instruct themselves in the mysteries of the life of the Lessurians. The first of these mysteries, which took some time to fathom, resided in the organic conditions that forbade an impure union of the sexes. Procreation and the sensual pleasures which accompany it require a sympathetic magnetism combining the vital forces in an equal embrace, in an equal love. Otherwise, the production of children takes place as with the Starians.

These physiological circumstances necessarily lead to the spiritualization of the passion of the sexes; but that passion, in order to fulfill itself, requires a perfectly sympathetic individual of the other sex.

From the age of puberty, each man begins to search for the woman whose vital fluid, whose lively force of sentiment, can enter into combination with the aspirations and needs of his being. The search is long. Often, only one woman is organized sympathetically with the man tormented by passion. Some are never able to find one; they become vagrant and melancholy.

It is understood that with these conditions and these difficulties, marriages must be made, it is not necessary to say apart from ideas of beauty, since the Lessurians are all beautiful, but at least always apart from ideas of wealth.

On Lessur, nature is, moreover, full of sensual pleasure and sympathy. Under the golden skies, in the lands of enchantment, and in the perfumed air, sometimes there pass showers of a fluid of penetrating effects, with currents of a voluptuous magnetism with mysterious waves gladdening all living and sensitive flesh.

IV.

It's in the vernal days,
When a cool wind in the trees
With golden sieves comes to scatter like sweet grain
A luxurious spindrift
To the amorous disposition;
When the flowers, not long ago closed tight,
Grandly spread out the brilliance of their attire;
When the four suns, facing each other in the skies,
Send their fires to cross from every ninety degrees
To the shores of Lessur, at times, over the land
Pass luminous eddies.
An unknown fluid flows level with the ground.
Those mild, electric pressures
Bring intense ravishments and sweet embraces
To all the transported human creatures;
It shocks, above all, shoot forth to them the touches
Of new, celestial pleasures.
Then, that entire world thrills to the measure
Of every jet impelled by a sensual stream;
And, then, all sensate things feel their nerves shudder
To the transports of a universal spasm.

V.

It would be impossible to give here even an incomplete idea of the perfection of the arts, and particularly of the visual arts of color and form. On Lessur, painting was practiced with a taste such that the Starians who had excelled at it—such as Mundaltor the Nemsède, who had cultivated it in the course of a long existence—could not get their fill of contemplating the Lessurians' pictorial wonders. The marvels of Lessurian architecture, however, seemed to them more to merit even admiration and wonder.

Beyond the beauty and elegance attributed to each monument in particular, the Lessurians arranged all the buildings in such a way as to give their palaces and cities, seen from a certain point of view, a fascinating appearance, making a bizarre or grandiose picture always full of majesty and originality. For this purpose, they generally constructed their towns in the shapes of amphitheaters on the sides of hills or on other sites picturesquely disposed; and there, with monuments, aqueducts, artificial streams, and artfully placed trees, they laid out a landscape, a striking and fantastic picture.

VI.

The Starians, charmed by the beauties of the planet, asked for and obtained authorization to establish colonies on several regions of that world. Lessur, being twice the size of Tassul, was proportionately less populated; for the Lessurians, with their aesthetic natures, were not very prolific. When they returned to Tassul, the travelers' report caused flotillas of *abares* to be chartered and to bring the surplus of the Starian species on Tassul to Lessur. Those multiplied in their turn under that fortunate sky. Relations were always maintained between the two globes by means of *abares*, and the descendents of Ramzuel grew and prospered amidst vicissitudes of less importance.

It was not until after another two centuries that the Starians of Lessur framed the project of adventuring once more into unknown space, hoping to find on a new globe other marvels to fuel their curiosity. That was why a squadron comprised of five hundred Starians from Lessur ascended into the sky and went to land on Rudar, the third satellite of the Starian system.

Chapter 3: Rudar

I.

When arriving near Rudar, the desires of the Starians, who had hoped to find a globe whose wonders would equal those of Lessur or, at least, Tassul, were unfortunately disappointed. Descending onto that world, the *abares* plunged into an obscure atmosphere and the Starians soon lost sight of the stars. The air surrounding Rudar was constituted of a kind of fuliginous fog, a gray mist without transparency, barely translucent to the light of day.

The Starians, leaving their *abares*, thought they would suffocate, breathing that impure air; thus, it was only after several hours that they could accustom themselves to this new environment.

The hearts of our travelers were oppressed when

they examined, in the obscurity of that sky, the soil under their feet. There were neither rivers nor seas, but only a land strewn with muddy lakes and swamps. In the sky was an eternal mist not pierced by any multicolored suns or twinkling stars.

Nevertheless, the vigorous vegetation everywhere spread out its leaves and branches of lusterless black—a uniform color, though sometimes shading into brown or into tints of saffron. In places, these plants were adorned with whitish flowers and, in the wintry seasons, sadly powdered with dirty snow.

II.

In the air, a blackish cloud
Draws its stubborn blind
Between the unkind, harsh ground
And the ever unknown Heavens.
From the opaque mud, the waters
Everywhere sink black pools
Or create blighted mires
Full of white and ashen demons.

No tree here does not trim
Its rugged trunk with a comb;
From the branches, the sharp rim
Extends its common slant.
Harsh nature without soft shades!
Great lichens, enormous molds
See their long shoots with black buds
Lost in the sky's constant night.

III.

The tradition preserved by the Rudarians reported that, in the earliest ages, the sky was dotted with stars, the air pure, the earth fertile, and brightly colored vegetation extended its branches and leaves. But in times that followed, continued the natives, the globe, disturbed by convulsions, shook on its foundations; the air became corrupt; the waters, dispersed over the earth's surface, covered it with swamps; and it was from that time onward that earth and sky, stars and vegetation became darkened.

IV.

Here is the description the Starian travelers made of the natives of Rudar:

These people are almost all tall, thin, and bony; they are endowed with considerable muscular power, and all their flesh, as if withered, is made up of grayish fibers, compact and strong. Their uniformly silvery skin gleams with a rather keen metallic brightness. Instead of hair, their heads are covered with narrow, long and glossy scales, to which the movements of the cranial muscles impart a sound similar to that made by rattlesnakes. Their emerald-green eyes have fiery, yellow pupils and send forth a singular phosphorescence. Moreover, their character is sad and taciturn, and their lives are an embittered and continual battle against a danger which nature has placed closer to them, perhaps, than to any other species.

That danger is *death*.

V.

Already for all, death is the unknown, the doubt,
The dreaded silence, vast and cold, the long night:
Death leaves our bodies to rot in the sepulcher,
Yet carries our souls far, we know not where!

VI.

Death, so cruelly real for all the races of men who succumb to it in the same manner as the Starians, is indeed even more terrible for Rudar's inhabitants.

Among the Rudarians, *death* is truly a living and visible being; the word refers to a species with the form and size of an elongated bladder, provided, all around its external envelope with membranes or hanging lamellas which serve as wings. Those beings, which have nothing in common with the other beings of Rudar, either in organization or in character, are for its human species and animal kingdom the ultimate devouring enemy and the end of all life; for the only food capable of quickening and sustaining the existence of the *deaths* is the souls of humans and the life-forces of animals, which the *deaths* are able to absorb—to drain at a distance—by inflating their muscular hides. Nothing but immaterial souls or vital spirits can feed and sustain them. Some of the *deaths* roving through the foggy air of Rudar prefer to feed on the souls of children and of young animals; others, on the souls of women; and others yet, in contrast, on the souls and vital forces of men of great courage. Some absorb the whole life at once; others, savoring the agony of their prey, first drain his strength, then leave him struggling for a while, but soon return to devour his intelligence, and finally keeping his soul for their last meal.

The Rudarians, with their constitutions of steel, would have been immortal if the fiends of *death* had not decimated them continually. However, for the whole duration of their existence, the energetic disposition of the Rudarians is in perpetual struggle with the objects of their destruction. The *deaths* themselves cannot be killed, except by the most scorching fire. That is why the Rudarians have invented weapons which, charged with a powerful fire, sometimes succeed in annihilating their merciless destroyers.

However indefatigable the Rudarians might show themselves in a war of this kind, the *deaths* would have long before entirely devoured their race if the Rudarians, all multiparous, did not continually reproduce and make good the losses to humanity by an amazing fecundity.

VII.

And yet, at times, this world of night and venom
Has its celebrations. Thus, when black with brume,
    In days of sultry fever
    The air grows heavier with vapor
From the lakes; when the night becomes more somber,
From the depths of those many bogs, one watches stir
    Hosts of will-o'-the-wisps,
    Greens, reds, blues and violets.
Then, suddenly there is a glittering!
The shifting trail of those colored fires, in dancing,
    Frolics, leaps, and sports.

The fires pass and repass,
Everywhere intermingling their blazing shades
And covering with light those transformed lands.
It is said that in those short times,
When those tremulous flames
On that cloudy world create a fairyland,
Mankind, bruised by anguish, is found
Forgetting pain and struggle
To enjoy themselves in the revel.
By the glimmer of those fires, and in immense groups
The impassioned people run to join in their leaps.
Oh! it's festival, love and joy;
For during those hours of the day,
Interrupting the course of their funeral feasts,
The deaths, full of terror, search for darker mists.

VIII.

It is especially in the hearts of those dancing tour-billons and amidst the intoxication of those festivities that are heard sung the praises and exploits of Ourbatram, the Rudarians' greatest hero. Oh! He was a hero such that the other races had never known. Elsewhere, those honored with that title picked it up in pools of blood; but Ourbatram, all his life, fought only those beings with glutinous and multiple wings which are the *deaths* of souls on Rudar. It is told that the *deaths* united in a legion to attack him and to attempt to devour his strength or suck out his life. Alone, Ourbatram fought against them for a hundred days and a hundred nights; but, at the end of that time, vanquished by sleep, he collapsed on a heap of corpses of the deadly monsters, and his vital force was immediately devoured by the famished *deaths* that had survived their companions.

Rudarian legends claim that, after that great battle, mortality diminished among the Rudarians; *deaths* became more rare for a while, until the deadly monsters multiplied again an the human species was again decimated, as is the case today.

Alas! the lands of Rudar have no more warriors of the quality of Ourbatram!

IX.

The curiosity of the Starian travelers once satisfied, they were eager to return to Lessur and Tassul, abandoning the plan they had conceived before their voyage of founding colonies on Rudar. Nevertheless, the reports they made to their compatriots about the unusual features of those lands decided several of the latter to cross space to explore such a strange world; and even today, Rudar receives each year the visits of a great number of foreigners from other worlds.

Moreover, the arrival of and contact with the Starians gave to the gloomy peoples of Rudar an invaluable benefit in teaching them the art of constructing *abares*. However, unlike the Starians, they could not escape their livid and unwholesome planet by that means; for almost all of them, once taken away from their fogs, wasted away and died. The etheric machines did permit them occasionally to rise to the superior limits of Rudar's atmosphere, and there was not one among them who was not permitted such ascensions—to be able, at least once in his life, to enjoy the sight of the stars in the constellated sky.

Chapter 4: Elier

I.

The discovery of, or rather, the voyage to Elier was a bold endeavor before which the audacity of the Starians of Tassul and Lessur long hesitated. However, its transparency and the light it reflects to the other planets strongly attracted the curiosity of the adventurous travelers who had previously explored Rudar. Choosing, therefore, a time when the conjunction of the worlds made the travel easier, five *abares* of large dimensions departed from Lessur, came to touch and refresh themselves at Rudar, and from there, audaciously launched out toward the distant celestial regions where Elier revolved.

The explorers had to renew the breathable air of the *abares* in the atmosphere of Rudar; but that air, thinner and less oxygenated than that of the other planets, corrupted so fast that it caused great havoc among the crews who had attempted that long voyage. A large number of the travelers died and, at the moment when they entered the atmosphere surrounding Elier, those who remained alive were at the point of being asphyxiated. Luckily for them, the restorative atmosphere of Elier promptly revived their lungs and quickened their blood, and they disembarked, in the number of several hundred, on the diaphanous new world which they had coveted.

II.

How utterly dreadful were those days of crossing!

Our intrepid Starians, wrecked in the ether,
Were dying in panting for a breath of air,
As mariners, becalmed on tropical water,
Would watch their thirsty throats wither with craving.

By their companions, the corpses of the dead
Were left to the void; and some of the moribund,
Who with their eyes gauged the abyss without end
Where every corpse took an infinite descent
And were near testing that immensity,
   Thought to know eternity
   By the depth of their interment.

III.

Those who only imagine transparency similar to that of water or crystal seen in our air have but an incomplete idea of the diaphanousness of the globe of Elier. The property of allowing light to pass through them possessed by bodies on that planet is equal to that of space or of the most fluid ether; so that, to the Starians' eyes, the stars then located at the nadir were perceived through the globe of Elier as if nothing had been interposed between the observer and those stars.

The arrival of the *abares*, of those opaque masses, frightened beyond all measure the animal kingdom of Elier, since beings from all parts of the globe perceived them floating at one point on its surface.

Upon landing on Elier, the Starians at first could not comprehend the general nature of beings and things on that world. The first glance revealed nothing to them but confusion and vaporous, indefinite forms. Their gazes, unhabituated to such a spectacle, needed to become accustomed, and learn to see different points on the globe; for the refraction of light brought to bear, according to the density, position, and distance of objects, dioptric effects difficult to apprehend by unpracticed eyes.

IV.

Plants and minerals, seas and atmospheric vapors enjoy an absolute transparency on Elier. Only the humans and higher animals stood out clearly above that whole by the opaline translucency of their bodies. Only their eyes, constructed like ours, were of an entirely opaque white. The muscles of that species have the appearance of fibrous fasciculus, of amianthus. The blood which flows through their arteries is similar to lymph; the veinous blood seems to be of chyle, or milk.

Despite a complexion offering in all its parts the vitreous appearance of a milky opal, the natives of Elier are large, agile, and well proportioned. Their women, a little smaller, are delicate and slightly diaphanous. Those dainty creatures, sporting extravagantly on the limpid surface of Elier, seemed to the Starians like so many graceful sylphs poised in the air.

V.

In this world there are no more colors;
An object's hue no longer darks the border
Of its external contours—
By tones of light they are depicted here.
The eye sees constantly
A thousand crystalline forms,

And pursues successively,
Through every object of those permeable realms
With an educated gaze, its endless
                    Explorations,
            Down to profound regions
Where the crust of the globe has its basis.
However, considering the geological plan,
One sees all formations are not without coloration
And that entire beds comprised of their layers
Reflect in rings the colors,
            The vivid hues of Iris.
This changing phenomenon explained to the Starians
Those colored lights sent back into the ether
Which made Elier admired from afar.

VI.

We have said it: the Starians could not make the acquaintance of the mysteries of that transparent world, except by degrees and after having been initiated by means of long study. The natives, accustomed to visually peering through the depths of space and their world's solid mass, distinguished marvelously, whether with the naked eye or with telescopes, the interior and exterior phenomena taking place in the bowels of the earth or on its surface, in the mineral kingdom or amidst organic nature.

On that world, composed of beings and objects infinitely varied and all of perfect transparency, it is the difference in the density of bodies which indicate surfaces to the Elierians' expert eyes. With the utmost skill, they can comprehend at a glance the forms of everything; and those forms, themselves penetrable, by no means prevent their gazes from comprehending, through the nearest forms, those of bodies which the first would have hidden if they had been opaque. Thus, an inhabitant of Elier, casting down his exploring gaze from the top of a mountain, perceives at first, on the surface of the ground, the forests spreading out a layer of diaphanous vegetation in dense tufts; and, thoroughly analyzing with his eyes each tree and each bit of moss, he can just as easily and distinctly study the superficial and deep strata from that point on down to the center of the world. His gaze, going through the entire thickness of Elier, can even, by means of a telescope, examine the buildings of a city at the antipodes—if, however, it is not forced to turn away before the rays of a sun blazing at the nadir.

VII.

When the Starians wanted to reside on Elier, they found themselves extremely ill at ease in the Elierians' dwellings, the transparency of which not only went against their customs, but even more so, offended their sense of decency with respect to the shameful circumstances of communal life. Therefore, they constructed with the *abares* a vast house which, instead of walls, was covered with canvas and furnished inside with tapestries.

VIII.

The Starians, encamped beneath that dark cover,
Received each day from their benevolent hosts
Bread as limpid and clear as the purest water,
Achromatic wines and transparent fruits.

The fire was about to go out; they went to a clearing
And cut some branches off a stout vegetable;
And the invisible flame, a ray of lightning,
Shot up crackling from that crystal fuel.

These people of Elier, with an opaline pallor,
Full of gentle benevolence, of friendly candor,
Overwhelmed our travelers with generosity.
From everywhere, on the Starian colony
There rained rich vestments of glassy cloth and lace
Draping their glazed lightness with brilliance and grace,
The most splendid jewels and crystalline furniture,
Examples of fantastic ruby sculpture
And flowers more dazzling with radiation than diamonds
In daylight scintillating like sudden flames.

IX.

Evoke now the winged inhabitants of the tenuous
and almost imponderable air of Elier: a whole invisible
creation of large insects, of ornitho-saurians, membra-
nous animals rather than firm and monadic beings—how
do I know?—vapors, effluvia which move inordinately
around you, responding to you with cries, with hum-
ming, with the rustling of wings and with incompre-
hended touches. When you hear all those sylphs move
and murmur at your sides, you search for them with your
eyes and scarcely perceive, at times, a flash passing over
your head like an arrow of vapor, less than a fleeting
shadow. The animate beings which fill the air, because
of the slight materiality of their structure, are the only
ones which the Elierians' eyes have not yet been able to
subject to examination. Thus, after some time on Elier,

the Starians told them the air seemed inhabited with dreams.

Truly, for Elier's inhabitants, to know is to see. Equipped with magnifying glass and telescope, they had carried the study of the natural sciences to the point that there were few organic mysteries for them. Happy the observers who could witness *de visu* the greater part of the natural phenomena of structure and of decomposition!

The state of the Elierians' mores derive entirely from the physical conditions in which nature has placed them. Virtue and austerity are necessary to people whose fellows, from one end of the world to the other, at every instant, can see their deeds and gestures. Dissimulation would be too difficult; and vices or the sense of shame are equally unknown. Natural men, they are loving and affable. Their character, animated by gentle and humane tendencies, can hardly bear the sight of suffering and evil; and, as each has his eyes on all, there is no unhappiness that is not consoled and no danger that is not instantly relieved. Among all these people, the law of Nature has made solidarity complete. Moreover, by means of a singular faculty related to their propensity to see and to become acquainted with everything in the world, they are endowed with a kind of common understanding, of a logic of sympathy which might pass for a *universal consciousness*. That is why opinion and faith always establish themselves among those people without contradiction, without discussion, and, so to speak, unanimously and by intuition.

X.

The travelers were charmed by the hospitality of the children of Elier, who willingly helped them to satisfy their curiosity. The Starians, who at first had deplored the monotony of the planet, in the end found on that globe and in the exploration of its life's mysteries a source of inexhaustible pleasures; the earlier monotony was changed for them into a boundless variety, which the practice of observation augmented each moment by increasing the immensity of perspective for the more assured and better instructed eye.

Nevertheless, a vague rumor which had soothed them before their departure from Lessur incessantly carried their thoughts back to their brothers on the lower satellites, for the idea of the whole Starian species returning to the mother planet had long been developing among their people. They hastened to return to Lessur and Tassul in order to join that expedition and to lend the help of their arms to the whole Starian nation, who perhaps were going to fight for their ancient possessions.

Chapter 5: The *Abares*

I.

Eight centuries had passed since the death of Ramzuel. Widespread on Tassul and Lessur, the Starians had multiplied to such an extent that they outnumbered the native races of those planets. However, an anxious hope or secret instinct had prevented them from regarding as definitive their establishment on the two planets.

On the contrary, the memory of their original home-land—perpetuated among them by the descriptive works of Cosmaël, the animated pictures of Mundaltor and, above all, the admirable poems of Séelevelt written after the flight of Ramzuel—at last inspired them with an inextinguishable yearning.

The Nemsèdes, who almost never left each other and who were, according to the Starian expression, the three faculties of the same soul, summed up for the exiled race all knowledge and all remembrance. They were the elder and superintending arbiters of the people. Through a thousand dangers, they had conducted Starian humanity from age to age to a perfect prosperity; but, thinking they had not completed their work of regeneration as long as the entire nation had not again taken possession of the homeworld, they endeavored to maintain in the people's minds the desire and hope of reconquering Star. Already for a century, the Starians believed at any moment they would hear the hour of departure sound. A song of hope, a hymn marked by a saddened love for the planet with a disc overwhelming them in its vast proportions, long had been sung on all the shores of Tassul and Lessur and in the intervening space crossed by *abares*; that song, attributed to Séelevelt, had fostered the thought of return.

II.

The Hymn of Séelevelt

In Tassul's fields covered with white vegetation
For hermaphrodites, o Starian, frequently,
When the brilliant birds make the trees all scintillation,

You gaze into space and search it thoughtfully.

Our home planet is richer and more vast;
> With more lovely skies and earth smiles Star.
Up there, our happiness waits, faithful and chaste,
> In the cradle of our progenitor.

Run through these flowering woods, which Lessur gives;
Listen to songs if inspired humanity.
These lands are scented—a gentle fluid leaves
Voluptuousness for your sensibility.

But our home planet is richer and more vast;
> With more lovely skies and earth smiles Star.
Up there, our happiness waits, faithful and chaste,
> In the cradle of our progenitor.

In the night of Rudar, our travelers explore
Its deaths, its will-o'-the-wisps and its steel tribe;
Or hurrying farther on to the colorless sphere,
They sound the secrets of a crystalline globe!

Go! the home planet is richer and more vast;
> With more lovely skies and earth smiles Star;
Up there, our happiness waits, faithful and chaste,
> In the cradle of our progenitor.

III.

It was in such a disposition that they found the man of immortal genius who then appeared. That man was named Marulcar. Noticed from his youth by Cosmaël, he first studied medicine and the sciences with the Nemsèdes; but, soon becoming equally the friend of the other two Longevites, he was the preferred student of all three, and, as they said to him, their son in spirit and knowledge. Following the advice of his spiritual parents, he resolved to employ his active mental powers and persevering energy in exclusive devotion to the project then occupying all imaginations and all courage. Marulcar, nominated by the Nemsèdes, was elected as the nation's director on the two planets. By order of the people, he was commanded to work ceaselessly toward a general descent of the Starians onto the mother world. Preparations lasted ten years, during which Marulcar, twenty times close to succumbing to the immensity of his task, the impatience of the people, and the slander of factions, was not able to continue his work except through the active support of the Nemsèdes. At last, on the eight-hundredth year of the Starians' exile on the satellites, on the anniversary of Ramzuel's arrival on Tassul, two flotillas composed of innumerable *abares* left Tassul and Lessur at the same time and came together in the ether at the upper limits of Star's atmosphere.

IV.

In the wide expanse, a million ships floated;
And their immense caravan advancing, suspended,
Seemed the Milky Way transported and descended.

V.

They moved along for two days in perfect order,
But then the course of their journey was troubled; for,

In plunging into the atmosphere as they gathered,
A movement occurred in their train; hurrying forward,
Some ships jostled each other in confusion.
And those bruised and agitated *abares* ran
Into the ranks below. Then, closer and closer,
All the harassed *abares*, trod down in disorder,
Broke the lines of ships in the path of their fall!
An entire world of voices sent forth the same wail!
How disaster increased as each tried to get clear!

It was a spectacle to inspire cries of fear.
The entire human race were pounding each other
In Heaven agitated with frightful disorder.

In the forefront, Marulcar saw the column founder;
He commanded, "Halt!" and his flag conveyed the order.
From afar the Starians understood the sign:
It was immobility, at that fatal time,
Which could save the flotilla... All stopped immediately,
And calm succeeded the tempest in the sky.

Delivered from their fear, the migrating nation
Reformed their spiral, and the immense procession
Wheeling, descended toward the ancestral land.

When the Starians' eyes could recognize the ground,
Anxiety gave way to ecstasy;
And millions sang the familiar melody.

Yes, our home planet is richer and more vast;
  With more lovely skies and earth smiles Star.
Here, our happiness waits, faithful and chaste,
  In the cradle of our progenitor.

BOOK IV

EXODUS AND DEUTERONOMY

I.

Submission of the Repleus

We left the Starian nation crowded in some one hundred thousand ovoid ships suspended in the middle regions of Star's atmosphere.

Now, it is on the ground that we are going to rejoin them.

The landing and reconquest took place without obstacle. The *Repleus* had lost memory of the Starians, but the stupefaction with which they were seized at discovering a race endowed with such noble faculties paralyzed their defenses and, everywhere, made them yield the planet and its domination.

Besides, the *Repleus*, almost intelligent when they had enjoyed contact with the Starians, once left to themselves had seen the brutality of their primitive nature regain the upper hand. By the time the Starians reconquered their homeworld, a great number of *Repleus* had returned to the wild—to such a degree that their former masters could not doubt that, if Star had continued to belong to them, the entire species would have eventually relapsed into pure animality.

Of the several kingdoms which still formed the *Repleu* society, that of Polymanie alone had the honor of being overthrown by Marulcar personally. The Starian commander, having heard by accident of the ignominious conduct of that idiotic nation, had the most extravagant Polymanians placed on top of a monument formerly erected in memory of some famous warriors or bloody battle and, after having them flogged in the presence of all the people of Polymanie, sent them to serve in his stables.

Those were the only reprisals that the Starians allowed themselves upon the species of which they had so much to complain. As for the other kingdoms, when the lieutenants of Marulcar wanted to visit them, they were already gone.

II.

First outposts.
General character and social instincts
of the modern Starians. Renaissance in literature.

After the conquest, the Starians' work on the re-conquered globe had to begin.

Of the inheritance of their fathers, there remained only the earth, the naked earth. The works of their ancestors had been so well overthrown that the sites of their former cities had become all but unrecognizable.

The use of *abares* permitted a prompt exploration of all the terrestrial regions and the immediate transportation of persons and goods, so the mass of the Starians soon dispersed over the greater part of the continents and islands, gathering in particular spots or particular climates according to taste and family affinities: some stopped in the neighborhood of bramble colonies; others pitched their tents on shores adorned with *celsinores*; all found their souls expanding in the warm rays of Star's multicolored suns.

Immediately, Star felt the hand of man again, and, in the months that followed, from east to west, new villages with hundreds of houses appeared.

Above all, the preoccupation was to live again.

When the cares of the first necessities were past, the people looked to their fellow Starians and social life began again. It began, in the villages or in groups, with the notion of equal and free relations.

The Starians remembered the last words of Ramzuel, who had declared proudly: *Respect my blood!* That is to say: you are noble, you are precious, you are almost divine—respect yourselves! Each drop of your blood is sacred, and each of your thoughts is intelligent; now, *make yourselves proud!*

These commentaries on Ramzuel's testament, developed and propagated by the Nemsèdes, had made of Starian pride the true spirit of the new generations, a time of mighty monarchs. The liberty of a proud human nature—such had been the only law of the Starians on the satellites. That law was written into no code, but it lived within everyone's heart. When Marulcar came to be elected Star's new leader, his genius had the honor, upon taking command, of summarizing this shared communal thought by inscribing upon the new flag: *Exaltation of Mankind.* That law, thus proclaimed, was indeed a law of Nature for the Starians; it was nothing more than the synthesis of the feelings which had dominated their minds and social relations for centuries.

Moreover, had even Marulcar, as head of the new nation, succumbed to the temptations of despotism, had he wished to restrict with laws the liberty of his people—whose just pride was barely reconciled to even the shackles that Nature and their own history had placed upon them—he could not have succeeded. He could not have ordained domesticity in a people too proud of their blood to want to see it turn servile and debased. He could not have ignored suffering and misery, when every Starian considered himself and his fellow men as precious beings, found misery degrading and saw in suffering an outrage against the majesty of his perfectible nature. And war! Who would be prepared to hurl themselves against one another—these people to whom Ramzuel, still full of the horrible memory of all humanity, gasping and butchered, had cried in a last sigh: *Respect my blood*!

Yes, truly, Starian pride was the first social virtue of a free Starian humanity.

Most assuredly, the ideas of despotism and slavery were far from Marulcar's thoughts; but a feeling of suspicious pride made it difficult for the Starians to bear the command of a leaders or a hierarchy of officers. Thus, when the insecurities which had led to Marulcar's governance no longer existed, he found himself by, virtue of that fact, suddenly without subjects and without authority.

Scarcely had the requirements of the first outposts been met, scarcely had several recently founded cities been able to serve as centers of intellectual development, than it was found that, among these people, endowed with the most lively sensibility, the arts and literature had been reborn, showing themselves in new forms.

At that time, Lesmirée was the city which mostly took the lead in the literary renaissance. Among the brilliant multitude who then flourished there, the poet Nelech-Gamar, author of several prized comedies, is cited. The concise form of this book prevents us from speaking of him to the extent we might desire, so we shall instead give a sample of his style, offering to the reader a translation of one of his shorter works. It must be said, after having had to recount so much suffering and adventure, that we ourselves are rather glad to refresh our thoughts in presenting one of the productions of that genial period of Starian history, when literature resembled the first smile of a people being reborn.

THE FORSAKEN OF LESSUR
(*A Comedy in One Act*)
by
Nelech-Gamar of Lesmirée

Translated into Verse Imitating the Starian

CHARACTERS

MIRPAS, a young Starian of Lessur;
NIFRASSO, an old man;
ILA, a girl.

The action takes place on Lessur. The stage represents a grove adorned with bushes covered with rich flowers. In the background, Ila's cottage is seen.

SCENE I
Mirpas, Nifrasso.

MIRPAS
My dear Nifrasso, I'm delighted that evil fate
Has left you forsaken here, as I. At least,
I am no longer alone. Though beautiful you're not,
Nor clever, still, an ugly companion is better than none.

NIFRASSO
In turn, I admit to you, great was my sorrow when
On that fatal day I saw above my head the swarm
Of *abares*, without me, climbing the skies to conquer
  Star.
A hundred times I cursed that brutal Marulcar,

Who didn't bear in mind having the late ones looked for.
Thus, having missed the convoy of humanity,
I wandered, hoping a similar adversity
Had fallen on someone else... In brief, the same misery
Held you here, when I found you in the nick of time.
My friend, in this deserted land where you've joined me,
I'm glad we've met; still, between us, I'll not disclaim
I was looking for another kind of companion.
Today, as always, I hoped to find, alone and forsaken,
Some lovely child that for a wife fate would have given.

MIRPAS

(aside)

What a cur, who, lost to all and without succor,
Goes through the wastes and into the thickets seeking a
    lover!

NIFRASSO

Despite myself, I'm always thinking: No woman here!
Most certainly, the Lessurians of these pleasant regions,
Seeing their globe abandoned forever by Starians,
Will send someone to populate these fertile lands.
Then, I know well, Nifrasso, so very sensitive,
We become the husband of some sympathetic nymph.
But those women, it's said, do not make love
Like us. I'm vexed, indeed, that women of that race
Would have in their husbands hearts of fare, but flesh of
    ice.
But maybe, later, Starians rising again into space
Will come to Lessur. I'll go with them and discreetly
    abandon
A beauty who can give only fine emotion
To go to Star to indulge myself in a more earthly
    fashion.

MIRPAS
(*aside*)
Amazing! Don't you know, you ape, you filthy old man,
That in half a thousand years, not a single Starian
Could touch the soul of one of those flowers of Lessur?

NIFRASSO
(*addressing the audience*)
Not a woman will come to show her pretty face!

MIRPAS
(*aside*)
He takes no notice!

NIFRASSO
(*still standing back-stage*)
Yonder I see a beautiful, shaded summerhouse!
A perfect order reigns around it. You'd say, Mirpas,
That it's not completely empty like others in this land.

MIRPAS
(*ironically*)
Inhabited by women, surely; it's much overdone!

NIFRASSO
(*returning with a distracted air
and his hair disheveled*)
Be quiet!… hush!

MIRPAS
Beg pardon?

NIFRASSO
(*with anxiety*)
Hush!
(*aside*)

At last, I've found
That single woman! Ah! I saw her clearly; she's there
Asleep beneath that bush.

MIRPAS
What is it?

NIFRASSO
(*in a hollow voice*)
Talk softly, you hear!
(*aside*)

So he learns nothing of my luck,
I must send him far; He'll ruin it.
(*to Mirpas*)
Let's go!

MIRPAS
(*aside*)
The dog is playing a trick!
(*to Nifrasso*)
No, I want to stay here.

NIFRASSO
Speak softer!

MIRPAS
(*louder*)
What?

NIFRASSO
You shriek like a horn, really!
(*aside*)
She's going to wake.

MIRPAS
(*shouting*)
Ah! that I could break your eardrums a hundred times;
But I want to shout—Tra la! tra la la!

SCENE II
The same, Ila.

ILA
(*hurrying up rubbing her eyes*)
Who could cause such noise in a vacant area?

NIFRASSO
All is lost!

MIRPAS
What do I see? A woman! Heavens, it's Ila!

NIFRASSO
(*aside*)
He knows her!

ILA
(*still rubbing her eyes*)
As I was sleeping… to have disturbed my repose—
The tiresome fools!

NIFRASSO

What? But aren't you completely amazed
To meet with us? Or have you fallen out with males?

ILA

(*after a pause*)
I now live very well alone, and it's without pleasure
I find you two disturbing my solitary leisure.
And Mirpas knows that, having once been my lover,
He scorned me. Now, in turn, I shall not see him.

NIFRASSO

(*aside*)
I take heart.

ILA

As for this old man, who so comically sighs,
Of all the hideous men I've ever seen, he's the worst.
Destiny had done better to spare me such company.

MIRPAS

Ila, I swear, we'll treat you with every courtesy.

NIFRASSO

We'll love you, even while lamenting your cruelty.

ILA

But why, while our whole race exposes itself to danger,
Did you remain?

MIRPAS

(*stammering*)
It's because of misunderstanding I'm here—

NIFRASSO
(*interrupting*)
It's necessary to decently explain the matter.
The day of departure, beautiful Oaï, at your rendezvous,
Was to have waited. But, suspecting her of deceit,
You had to run to her house. There, with no one in view,
Mirpas discovered, as the signal blazed in the sky,
That he had too long awaited the girl's goodbye.
The hour had struck. In haste, he returned to his family,
In hopes of embarking with them. But necessity had
  forced
Their departure; they had already left when he arrived
Home—too late. And there you have why Mirpas
  remained.

ILA
(*to Mirpas*)
Then, it was Oaï that you, Mr. Fickle, still love?

NIFRASSO
(*aside*)
Now he's done for—licked—I have all the advantage.

ILA
(*to Nifrasso*)
And you, kind old man, who kept you from the voyage?

NIFRASSO
Oh, I don't know.

MIRPAS
                Oh! him—now, that's a story!
He's sure his wife, who doesn't bear him excessive love,
Saw the chance of making her farewell definitive

To her old brute; and she took it. Nifrasso's fond of
  drinking.
The very eve of the exodus, while he was indulging
His passion in the cellar's depths, she, following,
Set about the deed: in the second basement then,
With two turns of the key, he was locked up alone.
The wine's intoxication in his old head was soon gone;
He called, he cried, but no one heard. He stormed, he
  swore
In futile rage. At last, when he could break out of there,
Everyone had left.

ILA
Really, that adventure is even funnier.

MIRPAS
(*to Ila*)
But shouldn't you, too, in your turn, tell us
Why we don't find ourselves here alone and forsaken?

ILA
Oh, me! It's very simple and doesn't make a yarn.
In this flowering wood, I was sleeping at some distance
When they embarked. Vaguely, I heard someone call for
  my presence;
But depression, the perfume of the flowers and
  carelessness
So thoroughly weighed down my sleep, that the
  following day
I still slept.

NIFRASSO
But after everyone had taken the way
Of the skies, left all alone, weren't you in great dismay?

ILA

Me? Oh, no!

NIFRASSO

Didn't anxiety or boredom,
Then, ever come to torment you in a life so lonesome?
But, what did you do?

ILA

Very often, I slept. It's a custom
I revel in! How I love to dream in the chiaroscuro
Of drowsing! I prefer Lessur to Star for that; Lessur,
Where the perfumed breeze, where waves of fragrant
  and pure air
So softly prolong that sleep.

MIRPAS

(*aside*)

The more I look at her,
The more I like her. She has, above all, a languorous fire
In her eyes! When she loved me, I never noticed;
That's singular.

(*to Ila*)

Tell me: why didn't I ever see in you
This passion before?

ILA

True; I used to sleep less than others—
A clue then that I was very stupid.

(*ironically.*)

I was in love with you;
So many nights were lost to sleep.

MIRPAS

                      Ah! how I bewail
That vanished time! I so much desire to have it still!
I would love you! Alone, you are worthy to be adored.
Come, Ila, I beg you to pardon my blindness, my stupid
    error…

ILA

Indeed, I'm most worthy to be loved; and, in this hour,
Since he can't love another, Mirpas offers himself as my
    lover.

NIFRASSO

You do well to be suspicious of that unfaithful man,
                  (*pointing at Mirpas*)
Who would deceive you. I alone in these parts, dear
    maiden,
Could know how to offer you sincere and real affection.
You'd be my life—

ILA

Ah, bah! you too!

MIRPAS

(*to Ila*)

                     Well, I'll repair
At once my past mistake, and I'll be willing to hear
Without complaining, your scoffing at my true fervor.
Yet, if ever you believed I had honor in my soul,
Let me swear that my loyal heart loves no other girl
But you!

ILA

It's unfortunate; but how can I not fail
To believe in a flame so newly kindled? Besides, the
   thought
Of my wounded dignity also commands me not
To listen as long as I have no rivals in this spot.

NIFRASSO

(to Mirpas)

There you are, Mirpas, this time you're in full flight.

(to Ila)

You see, my lovely child, I alone am worthy of trust.
My love for you could not be put in doubt an instant.

ILA

(aside)

How he eyes me!

(to Nifrasso)

I fear your approach; you make me worry.

NIFRASSO

Bah! One quickly gets used to ugliness. Well, try
To love me a little.

(amorously.)

I kiss your feet!...

ILA

You make me weary!

NIFRASSO

Under your disdain, do not think my heart flinches;
With a devouring fare, for your charms, it blazes, it
   scorches!

ILA

At your age, my kind old sir, such discourses
Are absurd. Goodbye!

MIRPAS
(*throwing himself in front of her*)
What?

ILA
I forbid you to follow my steps.

MIRPAS
But what will you do?

ILA
(*yawning slightly*)
I'm going to sleep.

MIRPAS
Again?

ILA
Mirpas,
Only love keeps me wide-awake, and I'm not in love.

(*She vanishes into her home*)

SCENE III

During the following aside, Nifrasso is seen in the background prowling around Ila's home.

MIRPAS
(*sadly*)
Is it really Ila? How amiable and playfully sweet!
How charming she is; I feel I could throw myself at her
  feet!
But, I've offended her, and the lady is obstinate.
What to do, alas!… But I have a plan…

(*He continues to walk about, musing*)

SCENE IV
Mirpas, Nifrasso.

MIRPAS
(*brusquely and with resentment*)
I'm leaving; I can't be subjugated to a little lady—
That's why I'm going.

NIFRASSO
You've been converted to that plan quickly!

MIRPAS
I'm going to try to walk to the nearest shore,
And if I reach there, then I will be able to wait
For some Lessurian vessel to chance by.

NIFRASSO
All considered, the attempt could be made.

MIRPAS
Are you coming with me? It ought to succeed.

NIFRASSO
(*with feigned hesitation*)
I walk quite badly; the road is long and very hard:
Really, I'm afraid I'd hamper you.

MIRPAS
Indeed!
You'd let me leave here alone?

NIFRASSO
Mirpas, doubtlessly,
You understand, in these regions of exile, all it costs me
To part with such a friend; but I'd reach eternity
Along the way.

MIRPAS
Well, if that's so, I'll take my way;
For this place is a burden to me, and I don't know why
I should stay.
(*he embraces Nifrasso*)
Goodbye, Nifrasso; and good luck!

(*He embraces him again and exits*)

SCENE V

NIFRASSO
(*watching him go away; with a gesture of joy.*)
Go away! And, if it's possible, may I never see you
again!
Ah, happy spite; and how well it's done!
(*gazing into the distance*)

He's beginning to run.
(*with transport*)
Now she's mine! Certainly, she must give a sign
Of a sweeter disposition.
(*still looking*)
I don't see him, happily.
Let's go! Now, discretion will be unnecessary.
Let's rout out the beauty, and let her feminine charms
Fall to me without delay!
(*he goes to knock at Ila's door*)
Open up!
(*he knocks again*)

SCENE VI
Nifrasso, Ila.

ILA
(*opening the door*)
Is it you, whom I detest? Where, then, is Mirpas?

NIFRASSO
He's run away on a nimble foot.

ILA
Mirpas is gone?

NIFRASSO
(*smirking*)
More than an hour ago; time flies; but I'm left so
You won't lose anything. See, even asleep, love comes!

ILA

(*impatiently*)

I couldn't sleep. What urgent motive induced Mirpas
To flee?

NIFRASSO

I don't know.

ILA

But, where did he direct his course?

NIFRASSO

Toward the sea, I think.

ILA,

(*aside*)

I was scoffing and inflexible
With him, and I was wrong.

NIFRASSO

(*approaching Ila*)

His absence must be eternal;
So, let's not think of him, only of us. My lovely girl,
A simple question is posed to us, in my opinion.
We're here in a great wasteland apart from everyone:
Not having a choice, try to love me, and we'll form an
   union.

ILA

Don't you feel at all how these speeches of a half-wit
Make you despicable? For my peace, therefore, I entreat
You to leave this area.

NIFRASSO

Don't see joking in it:
The law of nature, in bringing us alone to this place,
Has married us.

(*gallantly*)

And so, to leave you would be brainless.
I love you so much, I'm pressed to avail myself of my
rights,
My little wife…

(*he wants to kiss her*)

ILA

O Heaven! Help!

(*aside*)

He frightens me.

(*to Nifrasso*)

Don't come near me, for I fear you like an osprey;
My repugnance toward you is so strong that, in reality,
If I had to choose between you and an ape as a neighbor,
I'd choose the ape.

NIFRASSO

(*angrily*)

Well, too bad; in spite of your displeasure,
As to your refusing me, ah! here you haven't the leisure.

(*with vexation.*)

I'm really sorry that by my ugliness I offend.
Every mortal man needs a woman: therefore, I need
One; and, since, besides you, there isn't one in this
world,
It's you I need.

(*calmer*)

Dear child, let's reason correctly, then:
With a good husband, in a while, ugliness doesn't mean

A thing. In these vacant woods, you'd someday need
  protection.
Is it without cause that fate has brought us face to face?
If the Starians have, by misfortune, perished in space,
It's us that Heaven would have reserved to save the race
From destruction. In the name of Heaven, of humanity
Of which you'd be the mother, Ila, consent…

ILA

But really,
What are they to me—you, and the race and posterity!

NIFRASSO

(furious)
This is too much! Fate, with you, wants me to establish
The new species, understand that!

ILA

I'm under the lash!

NIFRASSO

Surely, I'll not allow humanity to perish
By the trifling stubbornness of your mind.

ILA

Well! dear sir,
If you must remain here, then it's Ila who will retire.
I'll flee you and to live hidden in some other quarter.

(she starts to go)

NIFRASSO

(rushing up to restrain her)
Flee! Do you think so? And deprive me, all my life,
Of a possession such as you!

149

ILA
Mercy!

NIFRASSO
(*holding her back*)
You'd be ravished with my rapture!

ILA
(*entreating*)
Pity! Let me go.

NIFRASSO
To live without—oh, that I don't desire.

ILA
I'm going to die!

NIFRASSO
(*trying to drag her along*)
Come, in your house—I want to have you.

ILA
(*with desperation*)
Mercy! But there's no one here to come to my rescue!

NIFRASSO
(*dragging her along*)
I have you—Come!

ILA
He's stronger—Heaven! what can I do?

SCENE VII

The same, Mirpas.

MIRPAS

You'd better let go, you filthy cur!

ILA
(*throwing herself into Mirpas' arms*)

Mirpas!

NIFRASSO
(*in terror*)

It's him!

MIRPAS
(*to Ila*)

I wanted to go, but couldn't.

ILA
(*further moved*)

Good, for I feel love's flame!

NIFRASSO
(*aside*)

He's lying, the cheat; his leaving was only a low
  stratagem
To compromise me.

MIRPAS
(*to Ila*)

Ila, yours is all my heart's fondness!
I'll marry you before Heaven, and on my honor, Mirpas
In pleasing and respecting you, will find his happiness.

ILA
(*naïvely*)
Take it—here is my hand; it still trembles.

NIFRASSO
(*with desperation*)
This can't happen!
Ah! but, permit me! for both of us, there's only one
Girl in the world; well, in all justice, let's see to the
    question;
In fairness, we must share her.

ILA
I'm laughing now: this graybeard
Is mad!

NIFRASSO
(*to Mirpas*)
Let's be reasonable. Without a wife, what life
    have I?
Could I live in these woods like a wild man?

MIRPAS
Come, quiet your anxiety;
For I'm going to end your vain, idiotic misery:
We, too, are going to travel to Star. Just now, when
Had I just left this area, I saw an *abare* wandering
Above. I shouted, made signs; and they, understanding,
Instantly descended. They told me that, after arriving
On the wonderful lands of Star, the active influence
Of several friends had the *abare* leave in a trice
To search for and rescue us, and our deliverance
Is at hand, awaiting only us—the crew is there.

ILA

(*with regret*)

But to live together all alone would have been so fair!

MIRPAS

Oh, Ila, I'll be your faithful husband anywhere.

NIFRASSO

(*to Mirpas*)

Embrace me! For my heart is drunk with the joy of life!
I'll plunge into sensual pleasures!

(*after reflection*)

But do be good enough
To take me somewhere where I can find a wife.

ILA

(*archly*)

Mirpas, I'll be watching you. I'll see that you refrain
From inconstant love. Tricks and evasions will be inane;
For, since I'm in love, I warn you, I'll never sleep again.

THE END.

III.

Founding of a new cult.
Revelation of the Nemsèdes.

During the time the organization of the new communities lasted, the triumvirate of the Nemsèdes retained only a moral influence over the scattered clans of Starians. That state of affairs lasted several years. Nevertheless, left to their own instincts, and without guiding principles to organize their lives, the Starian masses, in order to satisfy their minds and set down some kind of moral law, began investigating the remains of the ancient religions to adapt them to their present moral needs. The concern of the Nemsèdes was aroused by these trends, and they saw in them an immense danger for the morality and social virtues of Starian humanity. Profoundly convinced of the corrupting effect of certain forms of religious worship on the intellect, they bravely resolved to stop this evolution and made themselves the prophetic legislators of the new Starian nations. To those disquieted masses, who were searching for a god or a belief, according to their fancy, the triumvirate of Nemsèdes responded with this dogma, which resounded from one side of the world to the other:

BELIEVE IN YOURSELF.

Believe in yourself: that is to say, have no other cult than the perfection of human nature. Unrelentingly enlarge the faculties of those intelligent beings who have already subdued the world and who, by the progress of their industry, will, in the future, become a race of demigods.

Thus was founded the cult of mankind, a religion the germ of which all Starians already carried in the depths of their hearts. These tenets, moreover, were only the consecration of ideas that the Nemsèdes, for eight centuries, had sought to make dominant in the minds of the generations they had governed.

From that time onward, therefore, the peoples of Star formulated their act of faith as follows:

RESPECT, PERFECTION, DEIFICATION OF THE HUMAN BEING.

The Starians, having become fervent disciples of this natural and new human religion, the practices of which they drew from the instructions of the three Longevites, immediately instituted a priesthood to officiate over the parishes of the new cult in each community and in each group. These priests were of two orders. Some were charged with the physical instruction of mankind; they were the medical officers. The others were charged with mankind's education, moral hygiene, and perfecting; they were the civil officers. It was under the protection of this kind of theocracy that the newly-founded cities grew and developed.

IV.

Philosophical tenets of Séelevelt

The metaphysical and religious ideas taught in the modern Starians' temples—one might almost say schools—by the priests of the new moral order—at the same time judges, counselors and teachers—were due in large measure to the direction of the Nemsède Séelevelt.

The tenets of the new faith could be outlined in a few words:

What is, is one; that unity, Séelevelt called the *Un-created Panapérante*, which included three elements or manifestations: space, matter and God, the active and intelligent power. None of the three elements of the *Panapérante* could exist separated from the two others: all three were infinite, eternal and necessary.

Séelevelt rejected the notion of *creation*.[12] As for the human soul, the opinion commonly accepted by Ramzuel's descendants was the same which had been expressed by the majority of philosophers and religious lawmakers of Star's ancient world, and which could be

---

[12] Here are the principal arguments on which he based this: One could not conceive of absolute nothingness; that is to say, nothing in the universe, neither time, nor matter, nor space. Moreover, if one were to imagine, assuming such a thing was possible, that enormity, that nothingness, then, even if it existed for but an instant, one would then ask: where is God? That power no longer has a reason for being; it does not exist, nor could it exist.

Our minds, which by the succession of days and years, can conceive of a future eternity, can equally, by taking the present moment as a point of departure, count forever a similar succession of days passing up to the present, and thus generate the idea of a past eternity.

The idea of creation comes from the analogy which we unreflectively make between objects which surround us and the world itself. Everything appears to begin and end. Therefore, the universe itself must have been made like everything else. Indeed, nothing begins or ends in this world; for not an atom of matter, nor of physical or vital force is annihilated or lost. We see only the transformations of matter under the cadence of physical forces or under the breath of God, the intelligent force. Séelevelt asked: *Since nothing begins in the world, why should the world itself have begun?* (*Note from the Author*)

translated thus: After death, the souls of the virtuous become more sensitive and more intelligent and are carried off into an enchanted sphere to taste a thousand pleasures; while the souls of the wicked, losing thought and sensitivity, are dissolved and cease to exist.[13]

Our souls, Séelevelt said, are nothing but an emanation, an atom detached from the supreme intelligence; and that particle of divine power almost always returns after death to merge with the universe and the infinite source from which it was split.

Soon, however, Séelevelt, surpassing the opinion of the ancients, taught that the soul, through use and development of its faculties during this life, could grow to the point of constituting an individual force capable of surviving the dissolution of material elements. This soul, then, having itself become a supreme intelligence in turn, could resist absorption by the universal power, which tended to assimilate souls, and remained an immaterial individuality; in other words, the person, then, *became a god!*

To become a god—such was the goal of all intellectual life, according to Séelevelt.

These doctrinal ideas, which were very much in accord with the modern Starians' proud nature, traveled all over the world and gave a new enthusiasm to the cult of

---

[13] According to the ancient Starians, this earthly life is an experiment, a touchstone. God poured upon the earth all the souls from his hands in order to determine which merited life. Only virtuous souls were capable of living eternally. Evil souls, on the other hand, were broken up and became, after this life, what they had been before. This wholesome belief maintained by the Starians, incited individuals to virtue in order to achieve, through it, the perpetuity of life. (*Note from the Author*)

the moral and material progress of mankind. At its head were the Nemsèdes, who for a long time became the pontiffs of the new cult.

V.

Political Institutions of Marulcar

Some years had passed since the definitive establishment of the new communities, and almost all had prospered greatly, some in acquiring agricultural importance, others in becoming true industrial cities.

Marulcar, though fallen from supreme rank, had not ceased to be one of the most ardent supporters of the new colonization. Helped by a large number of friends, whose families had pitched their tents around his in an admirable location, he had laid the foundations of a city which became the most prosperous among the prosperous. That city received the name of Tasbar.

Since communication from group to group and from nation to nation were beginning to become more frequent, the entire world felt the need of a political organization to regulate relations and to centralize information and skills, and then to distribute them throughout Star. Nevertheless, fear of establishing a central authority dangerous to liberty, which each Starian felt within himself to be a proud necessity, caused the various communities to hesitate for some time in accomplishing the project.

The report of the marvels created by Marulcar, and the services rendered by this Starian Moses, designated him as the only legislator capable of organizing the new political authority of the reborn Starian world. Finally, on the advice of the Nemsèdes, whose doctrines Marulcar had embraced, the communities asked Marulcar to create a form of government which respected the freedom and independence of each person and each community.

Ceding to their request, Marulcar gave them the following political constitution, which, put to a vote in each nation, was unanimously approved and immediately put into effect.

Marulcar entrusted the federal power, supreme arbiter of international relations and of the political destinies of the Starian peoples, to an assembly named the *Chamber of Axiarchs*.

At the beginning, the choice of the Axiarchs, in the number of four hundred, would be made in the following manner:

A commission of delegates from each community named, by a plurality of votes, half the first Axiarchs. The latter, thus constituted, elected by selection the other half of their colleagues. The assembly, complete from that time on, would replace by a new nomination after a member's death the loss it had sustained. The choice of the Axiarchs could not take place except from categories wisely and carefully determined by Marulcar.

It must be noted that that dignity continually fell to the most distinguished and illustrious of men. The Axiarchs were very interested in selecting famous and glorious individuals, since their authority, almost entirely moral and relying for its power on the prestige of the names composing the assembly, would be weakened and lost the day they would deviate from the founding ideals to become a mere coterie.

Indeed, Starian history demonstrates that the power of the Axiarchs was more respected and absolute when the people comprising its assembly were brilliant and renowned.

VI.

The Three Principles, Foundation of Social Law

Immediately after its definitive establishment, the assembly of Axiarchs—which included Marulcar, some of his former lieutenants, and the Nemsèdes, Cosmaël, Séelevelt and Mundaltor—began the course of its deliberations by discussing the principles, or foundations, of civil society and of natural law.

The first of these principles, which first and unanimously came forth, acclaimed by every voice because it consecrated the free, proud individualism of each Starian, was this:

The independence of each in the respect of all.

At the time the Axiarchal power was instituted, Star was still in the early days of its second occupancy; each individual had taken from it what he needed to feed and clothe himself. The Axiarchs, seeing that property was excellent as a condition of individual independence and social order, and that it was a source of great satisfaction and of peace of mind for mankind, resolved to establish it upon a solid basis. By a wise and farsighted decision—and so that the first social law, *the independence of each in the respect of all* might be observed and find its practical sanction, even in the future—so that, above all, the present equality would not be altered and the land, the primary source of wealth, would always be accessible to the needs and enjoyment derived from its possession—it was forbidden for any person to acquire more than a set amount of land. Up until the division of the entire globe, non-occupied lands were to be reserved for the increase in the human population.[14] Thus, the Axiarchs set down as the second principle of the natural social law:

The ownership of land will be limited.

Finally, on the proposal of Marulcar, whose moral convictions had begun to come to light, a third principle was added to the first two. It was this:

Pain caused intentionally is an impiety and war a sacrilege.

The three principles of the Axiarchs, submitted to the approval of the people, were accepted everywhere and became forever the constitutional law of Star:

The independence of each in the respect of all.

The ownership of land will be limited.

Pain caused intentionally is an impiety and war a sacrilege.

VII.

Marulcar's moral principles. His tomb.

Marulcar's influence caused the Axiarchy to estab-

---

[14] The possession of a park or an orchard, said the Axiarchs who were in favor of limiting land ownership, can procure as much happiness as a vast domain; to taste the pleasures of land ownership, it is not necessary to own immense plains. According to Starian law, each owner was able to increase the value of his real estate; however, upon his death, that increased value was returned to public ownership, to be redivided more equitably. Other types of private ownership were, however, unlimited as it should be. (*Note from the Author*)

lish itself at Tasbar. Moreover, that great man, who was up to the end of his life, the instrument of the Tasbarites' material prosperity, had an even greater effect upon that people's moral convictions.

We spoke just now of Marulcar's moral convictions. Like almost all Starians, he was imbued with the Nemsèdes' metaphysical tenets, but toward the end of his life, he thought he ought to complete their work in establishing the ethics of humanity on its true foundations. His ideas were more particularly accepted and put into practice by the nation which recognized him as their founder. We will not easily understand the Tasbarites' customs and manners, which we will be reviewing later, if we do not first examine Marulcar's moral convictions.

When one seeks to discover the law and the motive for the actions of men and animals, said Marulcar, one discovers, in the final analysis, that they act and decide according to how they are affected; in other words, how they feel. Thus, man is first a sensitive being. He feels, and his pleasant or painful sensations irresistibly elicit his thoughts and actions.

Sensibility is therefore the source of all human morality. The individual, whatever he may say or do, avoids pain, unhappiness, evil and seeks pleasure, happiness, good. Instinctively, primitively, naturally, for animal, child and man, pain is evil and pleasure good. The perception of pleasure and pain is the consciousness of good and evil, which is the *criterion*, the foundation of the moral law. With man, reason causes him to extend to others what was the result of his own sensations and thus governs his relationships with his fellows.[15] He is moved

---

[15] Many say that conscience is innate in mankind for guidance in the practice of good; but, on the other hand, many also feel

by another's suffering by thinking of what he would experience if he suffered the same. From this, he develops pity, the sensitive source of the social virtues; the instinctive horror of his flesh, which shudders with fear, teaches him not to do unto others what it dreads himself and repels with all its energy, and, as a final corollary, to do unto others what seems to him good and agreeable.[16]

Human existence, in its actual state, has only two conditions, two manners of being: pain and pleasure. When the sum of pleasures or pleasant sensations is greater than that of mental pain and suffering, the person is considered happy; he is unhappy when the contrary occurs. Therefore, to banish suffering and to increase joy seemed to Marulcar the unique object of all philosophy and morality.

The Starian moralist then devoted himself to an examination of the nature and quality of life's pleasures. Here is a brief survey of his conclusions:

The satisfaction of physical needs, accomplished with refinement, good breeding and moderation, diffuses over existence a charm indispensable to that part of happiness which constitutes well-being, while the exaggerations and excesses into which we allow our appetites to fall are only capable of deadening, or even preventing, all feelings of true pleasure.

---

that conscience is but the product of education, when care is taken to make it an essential part of a child's upbringing. Conscience can also be the exaggeration of the emotion called remorse, and then is really something like the fear of the unknown, the most terrible of all fears. (*Note from the Author*)

[16] It is the suffering soul that has the most intense pity. The child is cruel because he has not yet suffered sufficiently. (*Note from the Author*)

The affections, friendship, love, and all the sentiments which suffice in certain circumstances for happiness in life, still can be developed and rendered sweeter through what Marulcar maintained to be the source of the highest pleasures, that is to say, through the direction and education of the mind.

The development of the intellectual faculties—that is the often repeated motto and teaching in Marulcar's book. It is intelligence and sensitivity which give moral grandeur to the affective sentiments. They give intense force and chaste delights to the emotions which enable souls to unite just as bodies do. For animals, love is the flesh; for the intelligent person, love is, above all, sentiment. Let us repeat it: education, in developing intelligence, increases in the same proportion *sensibility,* which is the *foundation of morality.*

Sensibility, which can overwhelm a person with the most intense joys, sometimes brings him its portion of pain and anguish. Above all, the affective passions of love and friendship, of an almost divine charm when they exist between noble-minded individuals, also can become the cause of the greatest moral suffering. But those pangs of the heart strengthen and exalt sensibility and make the person apt to perceive other pleasures more vividly.

It was, therefore, to those afflicted souls that Marulcar addressed his admonitions and advice.

The pleasures of the senses, the joys of sentiment, he said, render one liable to equivalent suffering. Unalloyed joys, on the contrary, are found in the practice of the arts and in study. These joys are exclusively the gift of education and exclusively comprise the intellectual pleasures. What is more remarkable is that intelligence and pleasure thus grow and are strengthened by each other. Intelligence enlarges the sphere of joys drawn from art or study; and study and art, in their turn, increase intelligence; and this happens *sempre crescendo*, up to the level of intellectual perfection and supreme sensual pleasure.

Would that we could follow Marulcar in his brilliant apology for artistic voluptuousness and the profound and calm happiness of passionate study! Perhaps, one day, we shall attempt to translate his fervent words which solicit and win one's heart to the cause of intellectual pleasure. We would describe with him the horrible spasms of the dilettante, the inebriating shocks of the spectator of a thrilling dance, the ecstasies of the painter before a masterpiece, the intelligent delirium of the poet moved by the splendors of a noble thought, the cool but sustained contentment of a scientist whose mind is incessantly discovering new wonders, and, above all, the ravishments of each sensitive person to the vibrations of the harmonies which spring from the earth and the skies, and which inundate him with their poetry. In those pages, the moralist yields to the artist, the only one, according to Marulcar, whose mission it is to instruct and *moralize*.

As we can see, the legislators agreed to put the Starians on the path of spiritual progress; the prophet Séelevelt caused them to hope for the immortality of the soul; and the moralist Marulcar wrote from a point of view closer to human nature; all made intellectual perfection and *moral sensibility* the conditions of terrestrial happiness.

In concluding his treatise on morality, Marulcar summarizes his book's philosophy, which is this:

What will be the natural and inevitable aspiration of human beings in this world?

The search for happiness and the cult of pleasure.

And what gives us happiness?

People, in general, achieve regular happiness though work. The select few may even achieve the most delectable happiness and enjoy the most divine pleasures through study and practice of the arts.

The whole law of natural morality is in these simple precepts.

Such is the summary of Marulcar's moral philosophy, which was wholly accepted by the Tasbarites and integrated into their manners and customs.

Upon that great man's death, which occurred in the fortieth year of the Starians' modern era, dated from the day of their landing upon Star, the Axiarchy had his tomb placed in the very palace where they held their sessions. That immense edifice, having become at once the Pantheon of the dead and of the living, received, with the statue of Marulcar, those of all the glories of humanity; and each century brought successively to that temple its share of statues of geniuses and illustrious officers of that land of intellect.

Mundaltor, who had produced the plans for the palace of the Axiarchy, on the front facing the east, had fixed in diamond letters the *Credo* of the Starians:

Respect	)	
Perfection	)	*of Mankind.*
Deification	)	

On the western front were the three Principles containing the Law of Star:

The independence of each in the respect of all.

The ownership of land will be limited.

Pain caused intentionally is an impiety and war a sacrilege.

INTERPOLATED INFORMATION

The books and manuscripts found in the heights of the Himalayas had belonged to a Starian named Sesello, who had gone to spend his solitary and studious old age on the slopes of the peak of Rerriton. These books were found mingled with personal correspondence which Sesello must have hidden in some secret cupboard, concealed in a corner of the rock where he had hollowed out his dwelling. A dreadful eruption of the volcano, which I believe destroyed it many years afterward, threw these documents encased in the rock into infinity.

By going through the diverse writings that fell into my possession, I was able to give form to this account and to extract the substance of this book's first four sections. What follows, on the contrary, is nothing but the word-for-word translation of a small *opus* which I found among Sesello's books and manuscripts. It is entitled *The Voyage of a Tassulian to Tasbar*, which to me seems a rather exact and very succinct survey of Starian civilization at the time when the historical data serving as the basis of this book stopped. I have preserved in the Tassulian's account two literary pieces which were found inserted, convinced that the reader will not be displeased to discover several samples of Tasbarite literature.

BOOK FIVE

VOYAGE OF A TASSULIAN TO TASBAR

What torrents of powerful and pure light bathes the land and the waters! What charm there is, too, in those warm nights, or rather those half-days that are successively blue, pink, green and purple, in an infinite variations of sights that are the poetry of nature! Truly, we are in Tasbar, the city that has the most beautiful weather of all the shining skies of Star.

How that city always seems to be celebrating! Wouldn't one say that happiness, pride and spirit infuse the very air and inflate the chests of its inhabitants?

The monuments, the banners, the decorations, the interiors of all the porticos and the streets, just as the faces of men, have a look of happy intelligence. It is indeed the City of Tasbar, the wonder of the land of Star.

Why do these crowds of people, smiling at the prospect of the pleasures they will soon feel, rush, some toward the temple-schools or the concert halls, others toward the museums, the academies, all seeking a noble joy? Why is art shining through everything man-made? Why this abundance of sculptures and ornaments, and these melodies that resound and follow one day and night? It is our daily life in Tasbar, the city of the arts on Star.

I left Avia, one of Tassul's main cities, after having long and tenderly embraced old Teusneuth, my adored *parens*, the unique source of my blood and life, and a crossing of several days brought me to the capital of the Starian world, where I disembarked on the thirty-fifth day of the month of Estrella, in the eighteen hundred sixty-second revolution of Ruliel, reckoning from the era of Marulcar. Like the majority of Tassulians who came with me, I lodged at a hotel managed by a compatriot and located on one of the quays bordering the principal arm of Trira, the river which flows through the western part of Tasbar.

Like all the younger generation of Tassulians, I had a rather complete control of the Starian language, which has, so to speak, become our own, and of the history of the Starian people. Nevertheless, after several days spent in Tasbar, I realized that I had to study more of Starian civilization's history to understand its present customs, to appreciate the beauties of its language, of its literature, and to follow the splendid development of its arts. The religious writings of the Nemsèdes, the books of Marulcar, with the Tasbanite moralists' commentaries, and especially the chronicles of the evolution of Starian race after the conquest of the globe by the *Repleus*, were the first objects of my studies.

When the Starians had left the lands of Tassul and Lessur in machines similar to that which carried me from my small globe to bring me to this one, they scattered by families or groups into different territories, seizing land where they needed it. The communities, almost all organized along the same model, then formed a federation, as it was called, under the patronage of the Axiarchy. But after some years, the majority, in grouping themselves according to their affinities, had formed several hundred little nations administered by civil officers of very limited authority and replaced by thirds each year. The duties of these officers were very simple, since the only law they had to interpret consisted in the sacramental formulas inscribed on the temple of Tasbar.

Each community, on the other hand, remained ever faithful to its beliefs and its original organization, with priests of two orders: the doctors and the teachers.

After Marulcar's death, the social influence of the three Nemsèdes, whom our parents on Tassul had regarded as the sovereign pastors of the Starian nation, was exercised only with respect to religion, of which they were regarded as its prophets. Those three preternatural individuals, to whom the Starians owed the most remarkable geniuses of their race—Ramzuel and Marulcar, among others—fixed their abodes in Tasbar and figured perpetually in the Axiarchy's ranks. It was noticed with a certain solicitude that they, who had lived nearly three thousand years, were finally beginning to grow old, and it was no longer doubted that, however much their lives were prolonged, they nevertheless would naturally find a limit. Each of them, in a self-assigned sphere of study, continued, as in the past, to gather together all science, art, and literature—in a word, to render more universal and more fertile the cult of mankind. Across centuries and generations, they had pursued resolutely and with all their strength this supreme goal: *the human made god*. Their presence in Tasbar contributed to give the Tasbarite nation the intellectual superiority which it possessed over the other nations. Let me also add that the eloquence of the Axiarchy, composed of all who were most illustrious on Star, made Tasbar the privileged city of Star.

Moreover, Marulcar, in founding this beautiful city, had marvelously chosen its location, the geographical center of Star's immense continents and the connecting link of the world map. Its position is thrice happy, for Tasbar is found at the junction of the two continents, on the shores of an immense sea, and at the mouths of three of this world's largest rivers—Trira, Saguir and the river most beloved by the Tasbarites, Lampédousiami, with its enchanting banks. These favorable conditions caused people to come here in great numbers, and several cities were founded successively in the neighborhood of Tasbar. With time, the expansion of Tasbar and its neighboring cities became such that all soon became intermeshed in one giant agglomeration;[17] thus is explained the present immensity of the capital of the nations recognizing the Axiarchy's moral authority.

Other peoples closely followed the Tasbarites in their civilized development. The *Pamisians*, the *Lesmirs*, the *Risdoles* and the *Mirélians*,[18] almost all descended from the Starian colonies of Lessur, threw an intense brilliance over the eminently progressive world.

In the histories of these peoples, there is not a trace of war or of spilled blood; the Starian law has always been scrupulously observed in that respect. Short-lived dissentions occurring in a few of the small states dis-

---

[17] Since it is impossible to place before the reader a world map of Star, we ought to say, for the comprehension of this passage, that the greater part of the two hemispheres are occupied by two continents which communicate with each other by the Isthmus of Tasbar. The city is located on the south of the isthmus and at the mouth of the three rivers—Trira flowing from east to west, Saguir coming from the northwest, and Lampédousiami flowing from north to south. (*Note from the Author*.)

[18] The Parnisians and the Lesmirs inhabit the western continent; the Risdoles and the Mirélians are peoples of the eastern continent. (*Note from the Author*)

persed over Star are of interest only to the political historian. Rarely did the ambitious attempt to change the government of freedom and independence Marulcar had set up. Only one succeeded in this—among the distant tribe of the Térépans.[19] That man, whose name history has never recorded and which is thus lost to posterity, having seduced several individuals with enticements of goods and gross pleasures, enlisted their support and, with their help, succeeded in gathering a troop of debauched and lost individuals, who formed a sort of militia. Thus constituted, the force helped their leader proclaim himself the absolute master of the state.

The Axiarchy at Tasbar, incapable of wishing blood and battle, did not arm the other peoples in order to overthrow that absurd government. They contented themselves with sending the Térépans emissaries who distributed among the masses an excerpt from Séelevelt's book, in which the Nemsèdes pronounced an anathema upon all those who made a profession of killing on the orders of a commander. The message was soon so effective that the soldiers, having become the objects of public horror, saw themselves abandoned by their wives and families and spurned by all as accursed. The general scorn opened the eyes of those wretches, who, to the last man, deserted their bloody flags.

Thus, the despot was overthrown and liberty restored be the dissolution of the very forces that had served to crush it.

Of all the Starian peoples, the Tasbarites are those whose mores best capture the philosophical spirit of Ma-

---

[19] A nation located in the north of the eastern continent. (*Note from the Author*)

173

rulcar's teachings, and they know how to most truly give form to them. The Tasbarites, eager for pleasures and, above all, for the pleasures of the intellect, devoted themselves to literature and the arts. The depositories of all knowledge, Séelevelt, Mundaltor and Cosmaël, charged with the supreme direction of religion, taught publicly in Tasbar's temple-schools. The taste for works of the mind became so general that the Tasbarites soon perpetually held the entire world's attention by sending forth every day new masterpieces as food for human thought. The neighboring peoples, ceaselessly attracted to Tasbar and anxious to participate in so much glory, asked to join it and united with it by acclamation.

This example was the signal for a revolution which took place in other countries of the globe. The divided nations grouped themselves around the most enlightened peoples, and the Starian world was soon reduced to a few states, which gathered further to draw closer the bonds of confederation, and to place everyone under the protective authority of the Axiarchy.

But what made the Tasbarites so well liked among the Starians was that they demonstrated to the world how intellectual pleasures could improve and ennoble the human race. They had showed how true was the new faith announced by the Nemsèdes and developed by their own compatriot, Marulcar. They gave proof to Star's peoples, who were already following their example, that the more the intellect is developed, the more the circle of human pleasures is enlarged, and the more pleasures become pure, varied, gracious and infinite.

Thus, everyone believed and accept with enthusiastic faith these few words, which comprised the whole catechism of their moral convictions:

Q. What ought to be the religion of mankind in this

world?

A. Intellectual perfection and the search for pure happiness.

Q. And what are the means of attaining them?

A. One attains them through study and art.

In the final analysis, it is evident that Starian history is scarcely more than the glorification of the arts, literature and the sciences, and that their heroes had to be poets, artists and inventors.

I will not speak of the scientific and industrial discoveries which have startled even our small sub-lunar world: for example, the invention of those vehicles which move by themselves, that is to say by the force of a coiled spring; or even of the perfection brought to the construction of *abares*, the speed of which can be increased almost infinitely without danger to the navigator. However, I cannot in silence pass over the discovery of a multitude of little bodies gravitating in the outer limits of Star's planetary attraction between the orbits of Elier and the red sun. Those asteroids, discovered a certain number of years ago by ethereal navigators, are not generally more than a few leagues in circumference and, because of their smallness, had previously escaped astronomical observation.

If that discovery attested to the boldness of Starian navigators in the last quarter-century, it still did not require the supreme audacity which the projects of our present-day navigators reveal. You recall that, a few years ago, explorers had already attempted to rise to the limits of the vortex closest to our great sun; but that, having reached the confines of the neighboring star-system of *Téléphir*, they bad fallen back, feeling they no longer had the power to go farther. Well, what those vainly attempted is now going to be accomplished, they say, by a crew of navigators in two *abares* of the largest dimensions. Other travelers, who followed them at an extreme distance, and who, afterward, returned, affirm that they did succeed in overcoming the obstacle and that, luckier than their predecessors, they penetrated Téléphir's vortex. But for a long time, the Tasbarite scientists and their fiends, full of curiosity and anxiety, have been waiting in vain for their return; nevertheless, some still hope that death will not have been the result of their courageous attempt.

I am now going to speak of the present state of Tasbarite civilization, the secrets of which a diligent study and a stay of several months in Tasbar are beginning to teach me.

I had come down to Tasbar to the establishment of a proprietor who, like me, is of Tassulian birth and who maintains commercial relations with our native world by means of ethereal navigation. The place is located, as I said, on a quay where immense vessels surrounded by *talersis* display the flags of their various origins. Each day, I would see, playing in the distance, the pennants surmounting a forest of masts.

The flag of the Tasbarites, of the people who have peacefully accomplished the moral conquest of the entire world, here adorns the largest and most magnificent ships. That civilized standard is composed of seven colors, which combine their hues as in the solar spectrum. These are, to be more exact, the colors of the rainbow shaded and arranged in the same order. The staff of the flag bears the white sun's image and the particular arms are indicated on a blue field where the sky's principal stars are sketched.

When you raise your eyes to that magnificent sky,

you understand that men must draw from it more than a mere symbol. Originally, in the Starians' written and scientific language, the stars had signs designating them. They were characters of abbreviation which were added to those composing the alphabet. Little by little, the numerical signs, which were based on the first letters of the alphabet, gave place to the astronomical signs; in that numerical system, the four suns and four moons—beginning with Ruliel, which is unity, up to Tassul, which gave its sign to the number eight—were joined by a star, which represents nine, and the earth, Star itself, which became zero.

Knowledge of the Starian numerals' origin gave me the explanation of something which had struck me the first time I found myself in Tasbar: all the houses of the immense city bear, with the numbers which classify them, the images of the stars represented by the numerals. Thus, the houses are said to be under the beneficent influence of those bodies; and it is a holiday in the home each time one of its protecting stars is, astronomically, in its summer or its perihelion.

The Starian months, each thirty-six days long, bear the names of the principal stars which shine in the night sky for the duration of each month.

For me, used to the coolness and calm of Tassulian customs, the commercial activity reigning in Tasbar's streets seems almost to resemble madness.

Upon my arrival, I set myself to work to sell some productions of my country I had brought with me to defray the expenses of my trip. In the exchanges I thus had to make, I was at first surprised to discover that all Starian money is of the same metal and wrought on the same model. All the coins were little metal plates, differing in value only according to the inscriptions engraved on them. The smaller coins are merely struck off with a stamp. The larger denominations include unmistakably the amount the state has assigned it and even bears the engraved signature of an officer of the treasury.

Nature has refused this earth, perhaps for its happiness, that certain metals be more rare than others. All are found in almost equal quantity.

Star's mineralogical riches do not confine themselves to a general abundance of all metals on its surface; they also include an infinity of fine stones, which, without real value because of their commonness, are nonetheless sought after by the Starians for use in works of art, the decoration of their houses, and, above all, as ornaments on certain parts of their costumes. Star's satellites have become, in this, the tributaries of the capital and furnish the Starians' jewel boxes with the brilliant variety of their own precious stones. Among these, the Starians seek above all the incomparable diamond of Elier, with its beautiful crystallizations causing light to scintillate in a continuous stream of rings with a rainbow-colored flame radiating from the stone's center like the source of an uncanny fire.

All these gems, as I was saying, serve especially for the ornamentation of clothing.

The Starians' present-day costume differs little from that which Tassulians were familiar with during the last period of that species' exile on Tassul and Lessur. For the women, it consists of a white tunic long enough to cover the feet and, over this, a shorter gown of rich material. Only ribbons are entwined around their heads and are arranged with the tresses and curls of their coiffures. The belt and bracelets are always composed of a network of precious stones and fastened with a carbuncle or a diamond of Elier. When Starian women leave their homes, they wrap around their heads lace veils with the two ends left free and thrown backward floating over their shoulders; a scarf of a transparent material from Elier is draped around them, enveloping them in its shimmering folds.

The costume of the men equals that of the women in richness and grace. Their long boots, coming up to knee, are generally of supple leather, violet-colored with golden tops or orange-colored with silver tops. The pants, made of a dull material, are almost entirely covered by an ample tunic belted at the waist. This tunic is ordinarily made of two superimposed fabrics. The first, of bright color and rich texture, is covered by a crystalline cloth of Elier or perhaps one of those gauzes with silver thread coming from the Mirélian manufacturers; only toward the bottom or hem of the tunic, at the belt and at the edges of the sleeves, does the colored material appear. A cravat of guipure, with graceful designs, lets its fringed knots fall over the upper chest. Finally, their city attire is completed with a large topcoat with wide sleeves and long folds, made of velvet or brocade, and a hat of the same material, but adorned with plumes, curled, flowing manes, and beds of pearls or clusters of small, brilliant diamonds.

The law of Marulcar, which places a limit upon the possession of real estate, prevents too great an accumulation of the fruits of labor, and sends capital flocking to the objects of art and luxury, since private property is unlimited. I do not think myself mistaken when I say that this is one of the secrets of the Starians' intellectual activity.

The territory occupied by the city of Tasbar includes, as I have said, a vast region. To the south is located the port where at every moment innumerable ships go up by the mouths of the three rivers into the more inland parts of the city. Gigantic canals connect the rivers' different arms across the immense developments of the city.

In the center of Tasbar is the site of the *abare* spaceport, providing regular service to the four satellites, but especially to Tassul and Lessur. More to the north, finally, toward the suburbs, one finds wide roads paved with slabs of hard, polished metal, which bring travelers and commodities from all corners of Star.

What torrents of powerful and pure light bathes the land and the waters! What charm there is, too, in those warm nights, or rather those half-days that are successively blue, pink, green and purple, in an infinite variations of sights that are the poetry of nature! Truly, we are in Tasbar, the city that has the most beautiful weather of all the shining skies of Star.

How that city always seems to be celebrating! Wouldn't one say that happiness, pride and spirit infuse the very air and inflate the chests of its inhabitants?

The monuments, the banners, the decorations, the interiors of all the porticos and the streets, just as the faces of men, have a look of happy intelligence. It is indeed the City of Tasbar, the wonder of the land of Star.

Why do these crowds of people, smiling at the prospect of the pleasures they will soon feel, rush, some toward the temple-schools or the concert halls, others toward the museums, the academies, all seeking a noble joy? Why is art shining through everything man-made? Why this abundance of sculptures and ornaments, and these melodies that resound and follow one day and night? It is our daily life in Tasbar, the city of the arts on Star.

The Tasbarite people leave at the disposal of their artists the treasures which they need for the creation of works. One could scarcely calculate the sums which Tasbarite architecture has drawn from public coffers; but one must add that Tasbar is covered with immortal monuments and the most marvelous buildings.

In general, Starian architecture is very diverse in method and style. Thus, I will speak here of only two orders of architecture which happily the Tasbarites have employed in the construction of the most celebrated buildings.

The essential component of the first of these two modes of architecture is a line broken several times, or a zigzag. One of Tasbar's principal theaters, the plan of which I have under my eyes at this very moment, is entirely of this broken style, always full of originality and fantasy. Of gigantic proportions, the theater uses in the middle of one of Tasbar's most extensive and best decorated public plazas. The groundwork upon which it rests forms an elongated oval circumscribed by a double row of columns rising in a regularly broken line and appearing to mount toward the cornices in winding. The walls are cut with star-shaped windows, which allow every evening the lights glittering inside to sparkle outward. Above the pediment and the roof, where the angles are everywhere harmoniously combined, rises the cupola, formed by a circular colonnade in which the columns, bringing together their parallel angles, seem, from below, like twisted cords hanging from the dome. The edifice is crowned by a long sheaf of lightning rods with all their shafts bent into zigzags, imitating the bolts of lightning while defying them.

There is another style of architecture which as yet has been used only once, but with the greatest success; this is the twisted style, the basic element of which is the helix or spiral line. Marulcar's tomb, having become at once the Starian's Pantheon and the palace of the Chamber of Axiarchs, is constructed entirely in this style—the most pleasing, most graceful, I shall say, almost the most voluptuous to the eye, that I have seen in Tasbar or elsewhere. All of Star's peoples wanted to contribute to that temple's construction, and they resolved to make it entirely of bronze. Its construction lasted three hundred years, and Mundaltor the Nemsède, who had designed its plans, supervised its execution right to the end.

The columns of this metal monument appear as spirals rising alternatively from right to left and from left to right, and support a vast entablature on which rest three enormous towers. Each tower, set off by a helix which encloses it from base to summit, in turning round and round diminishes and vanishes into the sky. The exterior spiral of each tower, that slope of ever-tightening coils, is itself bordered by a line of twisted columns. From the base to the summit of the building, the bronze walls are cut with rose windows and volutes, which allow light to penetrate into all its parts. Finally, ornaments which undulate and interlace above the capitals, turning in the opposite direction from the columns that support them, lead the eye agreeably among the harmonious stitches of a network of spiral, twisting, or flexuous lines.

Since I have entered the domain of the arts, let me say something about music and painting among the Tasbarites.

The favorite instrument of Tasbarite ladies is a kind

of keyboard harmonica. This instrument produces sound by means of hammers of a spongy wood which strike against lamellas of a dense, flexible and pleasantly resonant alloy.

For their public festivals and solemn ceremonies, the Tasbarites have invented a gigantic instrument for which they built, in one of the city's central districts, an enormous tower surmounted by a platform. Upon this platform stand the immense batteries of a colossal instrument, half organ, half carillon, the harmonies of which can be heard distinctly within a radius circumscribing half the city of Tasbar. The only time I was able to hear it, that instrument was being played by Mundaltor, who is regarded as the parent of the fine arts on Star.

Tasbar's museums are by far the richest and most beautiful in the world. I assure you that painting is pre-eminently the cherished and reverenced art of the Starian peoples, without exception. Ask a Tasbarite or a native of Risdole who he most admires in the world; he will answer: "A great painter."

How that art must be magnificent, but difficult, under skies which bestow on the earth a light so limpid, so penetrating, and, above all, so varied in tones and effects! What painters are these who can create such marvels on canvas—with the poetry of truth, in the midst of a nature of fantastic richness, of vast landscapes where the fires of several suns play—when, in a narrow frame, they must unite and reconcile the effects, light and warmth of those suns, which are often at different points in the sky, throwing their colored light upon objects, which reflect their fiery tints as if they were not illuminated, except through the stained-glass windows of one of our Tassulian temples! When I went to study the new masterpieces of the Tasbarite school, the crowd was pressing around a picture by a young painter, a student of Mundaltor the Nemsède. It was a Ruliel sunrise which, for my part, I found rendered with the most exquisite poetry.

On that canvas, the fires of the three colored suns have not yet lost the strength which the brilliance of the white sun is going to steal from them. Large drops of dew are attached to the blades of grass, or hang on the leaves of trees, and, according to the light they receive, they take on glistening colors and turn nature into a flowerbed of sapphires, emeralds and rubies. To the east, a supreme brightness emerges from dawn clouds. Opposite and in the background, in a bay, the shimmering sea beats the sterns of ships around which *talersis* move their fins. Finally, in the distance, the disc of Altéther is reflected, tracing a wake of green fire in the waves.

The collection of works by Tasbarite painters in the museum, where the most magnificent paintings of Mundaltor are also found, is considered by all the Starians as the most precious treasure of their entire world.

I assiduously attended Tasbar's theaters while familiarizing myself with Starian manners and customs. In making a study of the Starian theater, I came upon a pamphlet which described the theater's development among the ancients, that is to say, before Farnozas. In those primitive times, said the author of the pamphlet, fables were very popular, but the fablers did not think of giving them the form of little poems. It was their custom to arrange their fables as vaudevilles or little dramas in which they made animals, in the form of puppets, move and speak before the spectators; it even happened that, to augment the theatrical effect, people were disguised as animals and, along with these sham animals, real animals were trained to take part in these performances.

The fablers were, then, the first dramatists in the art's infancy. Little by little, drama assumed other forms, but up to now, tradition has preserved its edifying purpose; drama among the Starians, at least in its superior form, has remained an apologue.

That work on the origin of Starian theater gave me the explanation of some of the Tasbarites' theatrical customs. Thus, in certain smaller theaters, I saw *Repleus* playing roles appropriate to their condition. Those individuals were trained as actors and knew how to play their roles as *Repleus* in the same way the humans knew how to accomplish theirs.

One must not forget that the *Repleus*, as domestics, are most often involved in the events which occur in the private lives of families, and drama, which is preeminently a picture of manners and customs, could not dispense with them in its theatrical scheme.

Please permit me to insert here one of those intimate dramas, which I saw performed in a smaller theater in Tasbar. I have chosen it amongst all others, not because of the merits I see in it, but because it gives a rather accurate idea of the habits of domestic life among the Starians—and the Tasbarites in particular. Moreover, it will adequately replace what I would have had to say touching upon those customs and habits, and at the same time, reveal some traits of the infra-human species, the *Repleus* and the *Cétracites*.

THE CELSINORE
(*Starian Drama in One Act*)

CHARACTERS [20]

BASSAIL, Naé's uncle and guardian;
FIANOR, Nae's fiancé;
NAÉ, Bassail's ward;
GOUSTOF, a male *Cétracite*;
MURFIF, a male *Repleu*;
TOUROU, a female *Repleu*;
A *CITOS*, or blue domestic bird.

The action takes place in Tasbar. When the curtain rises, the stage represents a kind of patio. To the left and right are doors leading to several suites of rooms. The background, completely in daylight, is cut by two rows of spiral columns, and allows a garden of rich flowers to be seen. In the distance are the banks of the Lampédousiami, where there are scattered trees with orange-colored leaves. At different places, there are several celsinore plants.

SCENE I
Bassail, Fianor.

BASSAIL
Where are you coming from, Fianor? The white sun has run two thirds of its course. All our assembled friends have already played the prelude of the concert of your

---

[20] See page 178 for the costumes. (*Note from the Author*)

wedding. They are only waiting for you, to start the feast which will refresh their voices and kindle their verve to sing of your good fortune and of the charms of Naé, my ward and your beautiful fiancée.

FIANOR

The concert has begun without me, you say? Oh! Perhaps it is better that way, for my improvised verses in honor of Naé would not have been worthy of her. Only my heart and my love are capable of singing to her the words that will make her soul joyful.

BASSAIL

Was it the search for new wedding presents which has made you so late?

FIANOR

This morning, Naé spoke to me with admiration of a cameo she had seen in Lesmirée Street. After purchasing that jewel, I had the idea, while passing through the Square of the Axiarchs, to add to it some fabrics, figurines of Elierian opal and a miniature landscape representing a Lessurian city.

BASSAIL

And what did you do with those curiosities?

FIANOR

A *Cétracite* of rather vigorous appearance, followed me almost against my wishes and asked the favor of carrying the objects he had seen me buy in return for a small reward. I entrusted them to his care as a way of giving some alms to the poor devil. He should arrive at any time.

BASSAIL

Come on, come on! There is nothing today but happiness and love for, I tell you, I've discovered over there, under those trees with the orange leaves, the most beautiful celsinore I have ever seen. It has opened its rose corolla and displays its pillows of red stamens on the banks of the Lampédousiami. The first rays of the great sun caused it to open its curtains of perfumed petals.

FIANOR

Dear uncle, how happy I will be this evening! Ah! Here is my porter.

(*Goustof enters and puts down his load. After paying him, Fianor exits with Bassail*)

SCENE II

GOUSTOF
(*aside*)

Finally, my stratagem has succeeded. Here I am, introduced into this house—around which I've prowled many times when the sky was lit only by pale moons—waiting for the chance to enter it—seeking to discover whether the beauty of my life's mad dreams would ever show at the windows her face—the face I'd like to take in my hands and devour with kisses. Ha! It's her fiancé himself who, mistaking Goustof the *Cétracite* for a street beggar has brought me into this place where, if only I can see Naé, I will sate my eyes on human beauty and desires! Ah! If only some bold stroke could deliver that woman into my possession—the object of my fiery desires! But only guile or force could make me master of her for Naé, a woman of divine beauty has, like all the noble-natured women of Tasbar, a profound disdain for the son of a female *Repleu* and a degraded man, for a being who is almost an animal, that no one has ever loved... No, I'm lying to myself—Goustof the *Cétracite* has been loved. But he blushes to admit it. I'm loved by Tourou, the Repleu. Yes, that female dares to love me—me, with Starian blood in my veins! After all, eh! why not? Since I dare to love the beautiful Naé! It must be a law in the cycle of life that one must ever aspire to love one more noble than oneself... Oh—there she is! Tourou!

SCENE III
Goustof, Tourou.[21]

TOUROU
(*throwing herself into Goustof's arms*)
Goustof, my good friend!

GOUSTOF
(*rejecting her*)
Come on, come on! A female *Repleu* doesn't leap at me like a dog that's found its master. Eh! What are you doing here?

TOUROU
My brother Murfif and me—we're the servants in this house.

---

[21] The *Repleu*'s voice is small and sourish. Only her torso is covered by a tunic. (*Note from the Author*)

GOUSTOF

(*aside*)

I want to cajole the little *Repleu*, since maybe I'll need her for my schemes.

(*to Tourou*)

How you seem to have grown better looking since I saw you last! How soft and shining the silken hair of your fur, and how carefully your long ears are combed!

TOUROU

Today is my mistress's wedding.

GOUSTOF

And Tourou loves Naé, her mistress?

TOUROU

Oh, yes: Naé is kind.

GOUSTOF

And I, Tourou, do you love me as much as Naé?

TOUROU

Oh, I'd burn Naé to be able to lick you up!

GOUSTOF

Well, if you want me to embrace you this evening, you must obey me all day long.

TOUROU

Right; then I know you'll kiss me for sure, because I'll be very obedient.

SCENE IV
The same, Murfif.

(*Murfif enters carrying a* citos *on his hand. He is dressed in a tunic shorter than his sister's. His ears are shorter and his hair is rougher and more close-cropped*)

MURFIF
(*putting the bird on his shoulder
and his cap over his ear*)
Eh! Good day, dear *Cétracite*... Ah! I see you've come courting my sister, Tourou. You haven't chosen badly, friend Goustof: Tourou is more wanton and passionate than her brother Murfif.

TOUROU
(*to Goustof*)
My brother's right—if you want Tourou for yourself, you can have her!

GOUSTOF
(*to Murfif*)
Ah! truly, noble *Repleu*, you indeed have the tastes and appetites of your species.
(*aside*)
Alas! All too often, I feel only too well that I have some of that same blood running in my veins.

MURFIF
Really! I'm known to be the smartest *Repleu* in this part of Tasbar—and when I can get away from my master and go gallivanting in the suburbs! There's not a single *Repleu* that would dare fight me for the female I've picked.

GOUSTOF

Surely not! You're all braggarts as well as cowards.

MURFIF

(*insolently*)

When no Starian sees me, I'm not afraid of anything!
Got it?

GOUSTOF

Ah! Those *Repleus*! It seems to me that I'm here, myself, and I'm looking at you.

MURFIF

(*pulling back into a corner*)

Pardon, mercy! great *Cétracite*. Your voice has frightened my mistress's *citos*.

GOUSTOF

(*approaching the bird to caress it*)

So that's the bird who's bonded to Naé. Happy *citos*!
Every day you receive kisses from her lips.

(*Just as he goes to touch the bird, the* citos *repulses him
with its wing*s)

MURFIF

Cétracite, good *Cétracite*, don't cause grief to my gentle
citos!

GOUSTOF

Go on, go on! You can have your stupid bird.

MURFIF

Naé's *citos* knows me; it's used to having me take care of it. True, it's often a finicky master; but I like to take care of it. It—the *citos*—only loves Naé; it never sings, except for her. Well, despite that, I love that bird.

(*During this entire scene, Tourou has directed alluring looks at Goustof*)

SCENE V
Goustof, Naé.

(*Naé enters; upon seeing her, the* citos *flies to meet her; during this scene, the bird, perched near her, sing, in a melodious but small voice, songs imitated by the music of the orchestra playing with muted strings*)

NAÉ
(*aside*)

The banquet's last toasts have come—I hear the clash of the goblets being emptied... My darling Fianor has emerged victorious from the concert. His ardent imagination and his musical, poetic soul have been flashes leaving behind his friends' flights of fancy, so well inspired on other occasions. It seemed to me that my enraptured looks were warming my husband's verve. For me, and because of me, Fianor has shown himself to be more than a man—that is, a great artist. How much happiness is then in store for me, who, for the pleasures of my life, am going to be able to draw from the treasures of poetry, spirit and knowledge Fianor has amassed within himself—to touch in his darling's soul the sensible chord of his spirit's voluptuousness! What a com-

plete soul is his!
(noticing the wedding gifts)
And, look here, what a heart he has—what charming taste! How many galleries and bazaars must he have gone through to find such objects in Tasbar!

GOUSTOF
(interrupting)
This, divine lady, comes from an gallery on Lesmirée Street.

NAÉ
(turning around)
Who is this? Coming in, I thought I only saw Murfif.

GOUSTOF
I'm the porter Fianor hired to bringing home these objects, which please you so much. If your eyes could have inadvertently been lowered on this old servant, perhaps Naé, the beautiful woman, might have recognized a Cétracite who, once, on her father's ship, was the driver and groom of the *talersis*.

NAÉ
It was you who was in charge of guiding and taking care of the ship's cetaceans, for my honored and regretted father?

GOUSTOF
Yes. Oh, I remember these days. I remember, above all, a voyage you made with your father to the islands beyond the gulf of Tasbar, which they call the Cilléades. I almost let the ship drift in looking at you. As you are now, you were near me on the deck; and I sated myself

with looking at you. But you, goddess of the sea, who let your veils float in the wind, you did not see me.

NAÉ

My poor man, I certainly couldn't stop you from looking at me. But, myself, how could I have dreamed of looking at you?

GOUSTOF

Alas! It would have been better had you stopped me from looking at you—thus, you would have spared me the sacrilege I now feel toward a woman of your race. For, after having gazed at you so much, I... I love you!

NAÉ

(*simply*)

But, *talersis* keeper, in order to rid yourself of that un-natural passion, you no doubt recalled that your mother was a *Repleu*?

GOUSTOF

Yes! I told myself that I was like an insect in love with the blue sun. But, what's to be done, when this nature of mud has desires that burn it with all the fires of the white sun?

NAÉ

(*gently*)

Every woman, as you know, must treat with compassion and kindness the *Repleus* and the *Cétracites*, but she also must not allow anyone to draw her thoughts to things which may rightly rouse her disgust.

(*She exits. During this entire scene, the* citos *has sung*

*into its mistress's ears a music in harmony with the
thoughts she expressed*)

SCENE VI
Goustof, then Tourou.

GOUSTOF
(*for several moments, he remains
to reflect, crouching*)

Yesterday, I discovered on the seashore a nest of venomous scorpions; their sting is sufficient to kill even a *talersis*. I was going to clear the beach of those deadly animals; but then, I discovered in my heart so much poison and so much hate that I rejected that idea. If they crushed all poisonous beasts, I, Goustof would be destroyed before the scorpions. Therefore, I let the father and mother scorpions raise their family; and so as not to be generous by half, I even made them a present of the share of fresh meat that was my dinner...

(*Tourou returns*)

Say, my little *Repleu*, your mistress will be very happy tonight in her husband's arms, both of them enveloped in the corolla of the celsinore. Well, if you like, this same evening, open the door that gives onto the river for me, when the great sun has set, and I'll make you happy just like Naé.

TOUROU
Oh! Yes! Come! In your arms, Tourou will be happier than Naé.

(*they both go out*)

196

SCENE VII.
Fianor, Naé.

(they come out of the banquet hall; the citos *that accompanies them sings during this whole scene.)*

FIANOR
Our guests, so happy at the banquet and so enthusiastic at the concert, have now left us alone. To the two of us, a life of love; to me, your heart, treasure of sentiment!

NAÉ
To me, your thoughts, treasure of poetry, from which I shall long draw the sweetest enchantments!

FIANOR
You will always have all my thoughts, and my heart.

NAÉ
Darling, here we are united, both of us young and full of love. Life appears to us as a long and limpid river, like the one bathing these gardens—wouldn't you say that it ought to flow on without end?

FIANOR
That's strange! Your thoughts are full of tranquility and hope, and yet your bird's song no longer empathically reflects your sentiments—for it's taken a lugubrious tone.

NAÉ
(listening attentively to the citos)
You're right—I fear some calamity.

FIANOR

Come on, I was wrong to frighten you. Your *citos* is only jealous of the share of affection I will take from it. Naé, look at the sky! The white sun is about to disappear from the horizon; and already Star, illuminated by the colored rays of another sun, assumes greenish colors. Go, my sweet darling, lay aside these festival clothes. The air is mild and the nuptial celsinore discloses, over there, its down of stamens. I'll wait for you not far from it, on the misty banks of the Lampédousiami.

(*Naé holds out her hand to him and exits. Fianor also goes out, in another direction*)

SCENE VIII

A few moments ago, Ruliel set. The daylight, from the white it was, has become greenish, and the light illuminating objects is a bit less intense.

GOUSTOF

Thanks to Tourou the *Repleu*, who's let me into these gardens, my scheme has been put into execution. The two scorpions, nourished since yesterday by the meat I threw them as food, had not left their nest. Despite the danger, I was able to seize them and bring them here; and now they're sleeping amidst the cushions of red stamens in the celsinore which is to receive Naé and Fianor. Go, brilliant butterflies, disport yourselves in the flower's calyx! I will be there myself, hidden in the large leaves that creep around the celsinore's flower. I'll overhear you two embracing; I'll take pleasure in predicting your hugs, and my heart will burst with joy when, amidst the sighing of sensual pleasures, I'll hear the cries of anguish and death which will be wrung from you by the stings of my scorpions. They're coming! I'm going to hide myself into the foliage of the celsinore.

SCENE IX

Bassail, Naé.

BASSAIL

You're trembling, child!

NAÉ

Well... Yes, a feeling of disquiet oppresses my heart. My poor *citos* is sad and alarmed; and you know, you, my dear uncle, how its instincts are identified with the most intimate thoughts of my heart. This is the first time I've seen it frightened, when my soul is filled with joy.

BASSAIL

Your gentle bird is jealous or unwell. Go without fear to the celsinore, where your husband is to join you—go, my dear ward; your second father blesses your love.

(*at this moment, the* citos *rushes over to perch on Nae's shoulder and sings cries of alarm and dismay*)

NAÉ

Alas! What do the cries of this poor bird mean?
                    (*Naé caresses and tries to calm it*)
Sweet friend, is it your goodnight kiss that you've come seeking? Oh, Naé gives it to you heartily.

(*she kisses the bird. At once, the* citos, *as if it had waited*

only for that caress, flies toward the garden while send-
ing forth several notes of desperation)

BASSAIL
My child, set your mind at rest. And, a second time, go
in peace!

(*he embraces her*)

NAÉ
Well, until tomorrow, then.

(*she exits as the green daylight begins to diminish*)

SCENE X

BASSAIL
All is pure and calm in the sky. The stars shine silent.
The breeze that rises from the river carries up to me the
fragrance of the celsinore. This sweet-smelling air im-
presses me with my youth's most beautiful memories
and carries me back to the days of my greatest happiness. As at this hour, the skies beamed with hope. It was
there (*pointing a finger*) that I tasted the first charm of
wedding bliss—in that same place where Fianor, at this
moment perhaps, presses Naé to his heart! The nuptial
flower was fresh and rosy, and its rich petals and splendid stamens gave out their perfume as the savor of our
love... But I seem to hear cries along the river! What
could it be? Oh! I tremble for those children, and I
imagine some dreadful misfortune!...

SCENE XI
Bassail, Murfif, Tourou.

MURFIF
(*running up*)
Master! O Great Master! I just saw Goustof the *Cé-tracite* fleeing our gardens and jumping into the river, which he then crossed swimming.

TOUROU
(*on her knees*)
Ah! Pardon! that vile *Cétracite*—I loved him; I had him come for me. But I'll hate him now. I hate him!

BASSAIL
Go, you wretches! Run! Look for Naé and Fianor! Oh! Heaven, Heaven! What's become of them? I won't survive them!…

SCENE XII
The same, Fianor, Naé.

FIANOR
(*appearing with Naé*)
No, my uncle, it's not for us you should weep.
(*showing the citos, lifeless, that Naé
is bathing with tears*)
Here is the poor victim… Naé's *citos* sacrificed its life to save its mistress. Drawn by plaintive cries, I approached the celsinore designated to be the cradle of our love. I opened its corolla and I saw inside the flower the courageous bird dying in convulsions near two enormous scorpions which it had killed with its beak.

NAÉ

(*kissing the citos*)

Gentle bird that lived on my thoughts and died for me, your memory will live in me as much as my own thoughts.

MURFIF

(*crying*)

Murfif has lost his only friend! Murfif will die soon, too!

FIANOR

No, my good *Repleu*. I have, from infancy, possessed a *citos* that will become empathic to both Naé and I—and will be Murfif's friend.

(*to Naé.*)

Dry your tears, my noble wife, and may the night end for us according to Tasbarite custom. Just now, I found, in the east of the gardens, a new celsinore which this very evening came to open its virginal calyx to the pure rays of the emerald sun.

THE END.

This life passed amidst arts and spectacles enchants me. The Tasbarite customs, the air you breathe in Tasbar, truly invite savoring the divine pleasures the city offers you on all sides. And then—must it be said?—it pleases me above all that all opinions are free and without censors, because on Star, *thought is conscious of being free*. The Tassulians I have met here have lost the habitual coolness given them by the exclusive love of oneself and of one's blood natural to our hermaphroditic constitution; and almost all of them have abandoned themselves to the enchantment of practicing the fine arts.

Of all the travelers of extra-Starian origins, the Tassulians are, beyond a doubt, the most numerous in Tasbar. One meets very few Lessurians, almost no Elierians and no Rudarians at all. My host, the Tassulian innkeeper, who knew these different species through having previously traveled to their planets, explained to me why those peoples have never sent colonies to Star and have generally not mingled with the Starians after they had reconquered their homeworld. Could the translucent Elierians become survive far from their diaphanous globe? That seemed doubtful to him—and those who have come to Tasbar have been eager to return to their planet. The Rudarians, perpetually struggling with an unfruitful nature and a devouring scourge, may have wished to abandon their dark homeland, but those who landed on Tassul or on Star and had breathed the native air died soon afterward. It is believed that the bizarre constitution of that species requires the mists of their dense air for survival. With their magnificent planet, the Lessurians find no reason to be envious of the Starians' homeland. As for the Tassulians, who nevertheless come to visit Star in great numbers, their hermaphroditic constitution and their retiring character seem better adapted to the monotony of their sky and the perpetual mourning of their globe.

It indeed must be said, that, despite the intellectual pleasures with which I was gorging myself, I felt within me a kind of budding homesickness, that my host had rightly predicted. Moreover, the time fixed for my return to Tassul was not to be long awaited; and I wanted to put to good use the days which I still had, though being urged on by my desires to the moment when I would be able to see Avia again and to embrace the good Teusneuth, my *parens*.

I did not want to leave Star without having accomplished the pilgrimage every foreigner thinks obliged to make to the *Land of Rêvour*.

Rêvour is a still unexplored island located to the southeast of the eastern continent. At first, it seemed strange that the Starians, who have explored all of the worlds of space, were unable, to visit an island located on their own world. What I am going to say further on will explain this fact.

This land of Rêvour, the only one which is hidden from the scrutiny of the Starians, has, by this very fact, excited suppositions and exercised the imaginations of the entire world. Each storyteller, each novelist or poet has seized upon fabulous accounts concerning the mystery of that island, and today all the marvelous and magical in Starian literature rests upon fables on the subject of Rêvour.

I left in an *abare* with several Tasbarites of distinction, and, despite a considerable wind that retarded our progress—as you know, the speed of *abares* diminishes sensibly when moving within an atmosphere—two or three hours sufficed to bring us over Rêvour.

Nearly halfway, we had touched the summit of the peak of Rerriton. That colossal volcano, famous in Starian history, has not thrown forth any flames for many years. It is inhabited, on its lower slopes, by some philosopher hermits who have hollowed out their dwellings out of its hard, metal-like sides.

Upon arriving above the island of Rêvour, one is struck immediately by the strangeness of that strip of land. A zone of high rocks, like enormous crystals, projecting pyramids, all of sharp angles, is the first belt surrounding the island on all sides. This belt, in the shape of a circular band, surrounds another belt, a little wider, formed by a bottomless lake or chasm, where the sea rushes forward as if it were an immense torrent. The sea reaches this inner band through several openings hollowed out of the first belt's crystals, and after having circled rapidly the island's central part, it goes out again, through other subterranean outlets. The center of the island is the truly unknown part of it. An opaque and phosphorescent atmosphere covers all that part of Rêvour and does not permit passing travelers to fathom the mysteries it conceals. Although the makers of ballads and stories affirm the contrary, all those who have attempted to find their way in there, by sea or by air, have never returned. Be that as it may, that little corner of Star has made itself more spoken of than all of the continents and islands of the various planets of the system. Rêvour is the land of imaginary wonders. Perhaps it conceals nothing but a dreary desert; yet the imagination has peopled it with all sorts of monsters.

Since the agreed-upon time of my departure arrived immediately after my return to Tasbar, I said farewell once more to all the magnificence, to all the joys of the incomparable city and, on the appointed day, an ethereal *abare* came once more to lift me from the earth, but this time, to return to Tassul.

Only a few hours now remain of the crossing; nevertheless, to while away the time, I bought the poet Isrich's new work before my departure. After having read it, I decided to give it to my compatriots after the account of my transethereal voyage, persuaded that they would be grateful to me for sending them this novelty.

Avia, the thirty-third of the month of Ertaër, of the year 1863 of the era of Marulcar.

ELIA
(An Historical Poem in Prose)
by
Isrich of Tasbar

FIRST CANTO

What did this moved multitude wish? What did they
await in this place? The approaches to the principal opera house of Tasbar were obstructed by animated groups.
Some pressed under the colonnade, circulating between
the two angular rows of columns broken twenty times.
Others were leaning with their backs to the walls capriciously adorned with the zigzag's rhythms, which there
traced star-shaped apertures or fantastic arabesques. The
house doors, festooned with angular lines and day stars
like the figures of an embroidery, were besieged by the
waves of the multitude. Each was asking the others the
most recent news from the interior; for that, at the moment, full of masses of spectators, had left outside ten
times more of the curious than it could contain; and in
that hour of disappointed curiosity, the crowd standing
in the plaza of the opera house full of envy and regret,
had remained to follow the vicissitudes of the performance at a distance.

If outside the waiting was avidly curious, within the
spectators counted with murmuring impatience the minutes separating them from the curtain's rising.

All had the presentiment that a great work was
about to be unfolded behind that cloth. They had come
to attend the performance of an opera. The author's
name had renamed a mystery, but the leading role was to
be played by a woman famous and respected for her in-

tellect, decency, and immense talent in all branches of the liberal arts. On all the tiers of the vast hall, they were telling each other the history of the birth, life, and works of Elia, who, still in earliest youth, had already astonished Tasbarite society by her talents crowned with a fairylike beauty. Some cited her paintings collected by the museums; others recalled her first appearances as a composer on the subordinate opera stages; but everyone applauded beforehand her immense talent as a singer, which she had revealed on the great stage where she supported the magnificent repertory.

Elia, it was further said, was born on Lessur of Starian parents. Her maternal grandmother was a woman of Elier who, having married a Starian, had left her diaphanous world and had come to live in Tasbar with her husband. Elia's mother died during the voyage to Lessur, shortly after giving birth to her. Before dying, the mother confided her child to a Lessurian friend, who nursed the infant and fulfilled the other functions of a mother. She was one of the most distinguished women of Lessur. She gave Elia the education of her country's women: that is to say, making her a great poet and an inspired musician. Elia shone in the assemblies where, it is well known, poetic and musical improvisation is to give rhythm to the thoughts of all Lessurians. On Lessur, it is said, she was even sought after as a companion became of the charms of her dancing, that favorite diversion of Lessurian women. Her father by adoption, a distinguished painter, elated at Elia's successes, wanted in her to perfect the artist in himself by giving her art lessons.

Beyond her aptitude for the arts, Elia had further taken from that happy country the grace and aesthetic bearing of the women of Lessur. Thus, when she came to

Tasbar upon reaching marriageable age, to receive her parents' modest inheritance, she was taken for a sylph from celestial spaces.

At the time we find her in the theater, she had lived in Tasbar for three years. Her great beauty, her strange, almost ethereal physiognomy, the elegance of her manners—which one would have called entirely spiritualized—had from the first excited intense admiration. But her masterful ability of making the passions she conveyed on stage vibrate in the soul had made the classical land ring with the enthusiastic echoes of her artistic glory.

It was accompanied by these memories and by her just renown that Elia, the young and pure Elia, appeared to several thousand spectators. At the sight of so much beauty, youth, and soul, all those spectators, their hearts gone out to her: unanimously greeted her with a smile; each sent out his soul to her so that she could impart the transports which were seen already swelling in her breast.

The performance began with a profound meditation. The opera's subject was taken from the story of Starilla, the beautiful goddess of the Tréliors; and Elia was charged with representing the civilizing beauty of that ancient myth.

Now is the moment to sketch the outward appearance of this woman who concentrated upon her the eyes of several thousand persons.

Seeing Elia, one would guess her of mixed blood from Star and Elier. She had the transparent white coloring of Elierian women shaded with pink by Starian blood. Her light brown hair with golden highlights floated in a thousand curls gathered around her face of opal tinted with pink. Her eyes were of a deep blue; and her features, of an immaterial purity, clearly showed, in soft and flowing lines, its contours full of celestial grace. Upon hearing Elia speak or sing, one would listen with ravishment to her virgin's tone; and upon seeing her, one could not tire of gazing at her, for from her words or gestures streamed the poetic sentiment and elegant ease of the women of Lessur.

Elia summed up within herself art in beauty. Ah! she was indeed the Starilla of the new world—a living Starilla, thrilling the multitudes, this time not only by the exquisite grace of her form and manners, but also by the cries of her artist's soul, received by thousands of hearts beating with hers.

The first act ended amidst transports throughout the house, transports the furious acclamations of which, heard outside, gave birth to more and more numerous murmurs of regret.

At that moment of rest, when the performers songs and the instruments' harmonies were silent, while the still thrilling spectators communicated their impressions to each other, it became gradually apparent that the attention of the whole house was directed toward one box in the front of which stood a young man of great distinction. Immediately, the name of Abassur flew from mouth to mouth; and three shouts of admiration greeted the young man, the object of general attention; but he, whose presence had been able to distract the public's thoughts from the profound emotions which had stirred them, retired modestly to the back of the box occupied by his friends.

The small number of foreign spectators, questioning their neighbors to learn how this young man merited the crowd's acclamations, were informed that Abassur, whose name had already been remarkable in the sciences, had just become illustrious forever by bringing about a decisive perfecting of the navigation of *abares*. The speed of the machines, through Abassur's method, could be increased tenfold without detriment to the safety of ethereal travelers.

That discovery, which had moved the Tasbarite nation at the same time that the first appearances of Elia on the principal opera stage of Tasbar, at that moment, diverted the enthusiasm of the Starians, so lavish toward all kinds of glory.

When the curtain rose for the second act, the scenery's beauty drew the spontaneous applause of all those present. For the first time, Elia appeared in a ballet.

Elia, who had already put all the charms of her marvelous individuality at the service of the character of Starilla, here still knew how, through the progress of her dance, to spread out in all its aspects the pure ideal of human grace and beauty. Before those configurations, in which matter seemed no more than the sensible and penetrable vestment of the spirit and which held divine harmony in equilibrium, the entire house became transformed and had to adore it.

Oh! She was indeed a true goddess of beauty! It was questioned whether Starilla, a true divinity, but forgotten by human beings, had now wished to show herself to the Tasbarite people in all her splendor in order to recover her altars.

They no longer applauded: ravishment rendered them immobile!

The songs were heard once more interrupted by the frantic roar of the spectators, soon followed by a silence which preserved only the murmur of breath…

Finally the opera ended. All hearts were fatigued with the emotions of pleasure and passion.

After the curtain's fall and the dying away of the last notes of the orchestra, each remained immobile and silent in his place: the names of the composers were about to be revealed to the public.

In fact, one of the theater directors, who had followed the performance in a stage box, rose slowly and declared that the entire production, the scenery, the ballet, the poetry, and the music were the work of Elia.

When the artist reappeared on stage, the women waved to her with cries of joy. The men, without exception, bent one knee to the ground while sending her a triple volley of bravos!

SECOND CANTO

Amidst these moving multitudes, who were diffused through the streets of Tasbar and went getting entangled infinitely, only two men interest us, and when we perceive them, our eyes do not leave them.

Where were these two young men going as they walked side by side through the vast circuitous roads of the Tasbarite city, along palaces where the marvels of industry were displayed—so occupied with their private conversation that they neither saw nor heard what was taking place along their way? One of them is already known to us by having been observed yesterday, at the first performance of *Starilla*; he is Abassur, the scientist, the intrepid traveler for whom space, the infinity of the skies, no longer existed. His friend's name is Glaïmir. He was one of the small number of Elia's distant relatives; and that title permitted him sometimes to approach her—she who was at the moment the admiration of Star's capital.

212

They were walking; they proceeded always talking. Where, then, were they going?

It is customary, as is well known, in the literary and artistic world, that on the day after a success, the friends of the composers and interpreters of the new piece go to the foyer of the theater there to compliment those who have well merited notoriety. It was to this ceremony that Abassur came led by Glaïmir, desirous of presenting him to his relation.

They were going; they were proceeding through the intricacies of the streets; and Glaïmir, as he walked, could not refrain from relinquishing all his thoughts to the bosom of his friend. Glaïmir was recounting the impression his heart had always preserved of the first sudden appearance amidst his family made by Elia, beautiful, poor, and touching, arriving from Lessur to request her father's inheritance from her relations.

"I was young," he said; "no woman had yet arrested my gaze. My eyes engraved in my soul the image of Elia; and since then, I've never looked at another woman."

"Elia is a great artist," replied Abassur, "for yesterday, in listening to her, for the first time in my life, I was conscious of being moved by a peaceful emotion. Continue, Glaïmir, to love Elia, since she is the girl who has gladdened your heart with the first sentiment of tenderness. I'm little versed in the study of human passions, but I believe in the endurance, in the perpetuity, of first love, of the new and pure sentiment that a young, simple, and sensitive woman has caused to be born in you. Myself, amidst the painful studies and arid labors of my whole life, I've always felt my inattentive mind carried back with happiness to her to whom my child's heart was given, and who, on her part, also has dedicated to me an almost prepubescent love, and all with naive unreservedness. You've seen Nérillis at my father's. She was brought there and raised with my sisters when she lost her father, my mother's uncle. Unknown to her, grace is in her whole person; the frankness of her heart shines in her looks. Well, it is to her that I've owed the calm and serenity of my soul in the middle of my work. It was through her love, the amiable satisfaction given to the needs of my heart, perhaps that I was able to avert idleness, which would have delayed the difficult studies that I've known."

"Don't you well know, Abassur," interrupted Glaïmir, "that I ardently envy the fame you've been able to conquer? I'm ashamed of not being able to offer Elia—my veneration contending with twenty of the most brilliant rivals—anything but a name belonging to a doubtlessly glorious family, but which I've not been able to rejuvenate with a new luster."

"What does that matter? If Elia loves you, she'll be happy to raise you to her level, as I'll be happy to give my name to Nérillis."

They had been walking for a long time jostling the crowd; but at that instant, Glaïmir stopped: they found themselves at the door of one of the museums which contained some of Elia's paintings. Glaïmir had Abassur go in. The latter, who until then had little examined Elia's different works, was struck by the vigor and poetic composition of the young artist's pictures. His ecstatic admiration would have kept him a long time devouring those suave paintings with his eyes, if Glaïmir, recalling that Elia perhaps would not find them the first to congratulate her, had not dragged his friend along with him.

They left then and went running to the theater, despite the hindrance of traffic where there crossed a multitude of people, riders, *Repleus* and vehicles.

When they entered the hall where the festivity in Elia's honor was to be held, she had not yet appeared. Abassur, upon entering, found himself quickly surrounded by the elite of illustrious Starians who had made an appointment there. But the artist, the object of the ceremony, made her entrance, and the press that had surrounded Abassur made a circle around her.

The girl's face, prototype of the most exquisite beauty, then reflected elation and joy. Elia, at that moment, truly could have represented, in the eyes of those present, the myth, the divinity, of happiness. Whoever would have been able to detach his gaze from her in order to carry it back to the entourage of the most lovely Starians, a multitude of whom filled the hall, would have been tempted to believe that, with her slender, soft, and unblemished form and features and celestial grace, this woman was of a more than human essence.

Soon, testimonies of respectful enthusiasm burst out on all sides. The young men, especially those who had already acquired some distinction and who were much envied, brought to Elia's feet homage in which one could clearly catch a glimpse of a passion more intense than their admiration for the woman or for the artist. Around her pressed Teuzesful, Noraïl, Vallaës and Daëllim, all names known and venerated by the Tasbarites.

Glaïmir, the most earnest of Elia's suitors, had, as her closest relative, the privilege of entertaining her in particular and of accompanying her when she went through the ranks of young women, whom she thanked effusively for having come to attend the festivity given in response to *Starilla*'s success.

Upon entering the fashionable circles, Elia had seen the crowd's welcome of the young and modest Abassur. She could not refrain from congratulating Glaïmir for being counted among the friends of that man of great genius. Glaïmir, encouraged by Elia's words, asked her permission to present Abassur to her, and immediately going to bring his friend, he led him to Elia and, for the moment, surrendered to him the honor of being her escort.

When the crowd that filled the drawing rooms saw Abassur take Elia's arm, they respectfully made way for the two young people. A murmur of satisfaction was heard, as if each of them had felt that Elia's high soul alone could be equal to the stature of Abassur's mighty intellect. The exigencies and etiquette of the festivity prevented the conversation of Abassur and Elia from being much prolonged; but they both received from it a profound, although different, impression.

Elia's heart, until then entirely possessed by a passion for the arts, felt shaken within itself by confused spasms of sadness and disquiet, precursors of the tender passions.

As for Abassur, the dances and songs of the night before, the contemplation of Elia's paintings at the museum, and, further, just now, that conversation all scintillating with the poetic spirit of the young woman whose harmoniously sounded words still vibrated in his ear had opened his soul to joys which until then he had not suspected. Elia had made spring forth in him the fountain where his spirit plentifully and delightfully drank intense waves of pleasure and clear happiness.

The festivity ended with a recital in which Elia was heard.

Her songs had ceased a moment ago, and the multitude was listening full of joy and effusion, when Abassur, immobile in his seat, again felt all his faculties enchained, suspended by the melodies modulated by Elia's sweet voice.

Abassur returned to his father's home still moved and surprised by the new sensations which since the day before had caused to thrill in him a divine pleasure. It required nothing less than the naive disquiet and the touching attentions of the amiable Nérillis to draw him out of the reverie into which those emotions had thrown him.

THIRD CANTO

When Elia returned to her modest home, she began to muse, then cast her eyes around her, and this time felt the dark cold of nothingness. This time, she did not have a word or a caressing smile for her two faithful *Repleus*, the intelligent Vanoumi and the energetic Flaousta. In the look of supreme investigation she cast into her heart, she saw that a passion was being born and that Abassur was its object; and, although she foresaw all that love could hold for her in future pain and anguish, she still did not seek to drive it from her. Although Abassur was perhaps the most sought after man in Tasbar, Elia it must be said, vowed aloud that she was worthy of him.

Several days passed during which the young artist let herself slide indolently along in love's gilded dreams. At last, her nascent passion made her forget art; she no longer either painted or composed. Even *Starilla*, after three times arousing the Tasbarite public's frenetic enthusiasm, had ceased her songs. Alas! if she could have known that, while she was forgetting her cherished arts to let her spirit roam through an imaginary Eden full of Abassur's love, he was spending every moment near Nérillis, whose pure love sufficed his emotions and filled his heart.

Nevertheless, even at the feet of Nérillis, Abassur thought often of Elia. But that thought was nothing other than the memory of an intense enjoyment, of an entirely delightful state of the soul for which he thirsted intellectually. To Nérillis, he read Elia's most beautiful poetry. He dragged her through all the museums to have her admire the supreme artist's paintings. More than anyone else, Abassur suffered from Elia's silence. He questioned Glaïmir about the motives of her seclusion. He would have wished, like Glaïmir, to be able to approach to ask her for her dances, her songs, and the work of her brush—in a word, the pleasure, the sweet voluptuousness of the intellect, with which she had once elated him.

Tormented by unsatisfied desires, he was fond of traveling alone in the mountains or in the heart of forests along the river Saguir's banks. There, he amused himself with watching the highly sensitive *bramiles* moving their limbs, or else making those animal-plants flee through the air employing their leaves as wings. At other times, with his back to the colossal wall of a *syphus* trunk, he would listen, through the din and rumbling of the wind in the branches of the immense vegetable which moved above his head, to the distant metallic sounds of the *lartimor*'s dry fruit. It seemed to him that the cadenced and harmonious notes the wind brought to him recalled the moving melodies he had heard from Elia's lips.

Meanwhile, the whole literary and artistic world of Tasbar also murmured against the voluntary reclusion of Elia. Finally, she, vanquished by the multitude's importunity, consented to be heard at a concert given by a new Axiarch to celebrate his elevation to the Starians' supreme civil office. The announcement of Elia's reappearance in public made Abassur thrill with expectation. In his eager anxiety, he had used his name and influence to be seated in the first row, so that upon entering into the circle reserved to the performers, Elia, in her turn, could see the present object of all her thoughts.

Each time Elia showed herself and even before she let fall a single note, everyone, except Abassur perhaps, was under the influence of her angelic beauty. But when she had begun to make herself heard, Elia, who had perceived Abassur's indifference, remarked with visible satisfaction the applause which her melodies, exalted by a vigorous poetic sense, drew from the man of her choice. From that time, her inspiration took on new life; her spirit was ignited at the burning furnace of her heart. Abassur loved her songs and poetry; Elia, at that hour, therefore, conceived the project of captivating the scientist's mind, of winning it over, of subduing it to herself by voluptuously intoxicating it with the poetic emanations which increased her faculties and overflowed from her artist's soul. She told herself that Abassur would belong to her when she would be able to pour into him the wont of spiritual pleasures her genius had the ability to bestow on the multitude.

Thus, from that moment, Elia directed toward Abassur the magnetic jet of her creative soul. Moreover, love gave her new abilities. Each day a piece of poetry, a picture, a statue came from her hands. In the theater, her creations, which multiplied, did not even allow the public, eager for those divine pleasures, time to long for their intellectual food. Of all those voluptuous spirits, Abassur showed himself the most eager and most passionate. She guessed him each day more and more affected by the enchantment with which she enclosed him. Indeed, Abassur's faculties, augmented and identified with Elia's, would receive from the woman artist's inspirations, shocks of incorporeal voluptuousness. At that sublime school, Abassur had ended by feeling as much as anyone; truly, he himself had become one of those spirits with the power to create and had given Elia homage in several pleasing productions; in a word, at a breath from Elia's soul, Abassur had become a great artist.

Oh! It was a time of rapture and enthusiastic delights in which the awed multitude ran to receive from those two inspired ones the sweetest emotions and to attend the tournament of inspiration in which Abassur sparkled beside Elia, while flashes of inspiration burst from the latter in a way that inflamed her lover's soul. They gave up their faculties and gathered the transports of the spirit. Abassur had become a poet, but Elia's poetry manifested itself in all art forms. Painting, music, and dance were other languages which she knew how to handle with success.

Glaïmir, carried away like the rest in that torrent of artistic pleasure, had retained, however, sufficient reflective power to discover that Abassur was the man Elia loved and the object of that flood of poetry. When his doubts were changed into certainty, his soul, expanding in the sweetness of the arts, contracted within him, and jealousy soon completely possessed him. Admitted into the intimacy of Abassur's family, he hurried to the women's apartment where Nérillis, abandoned for art and poetry, poured out her repining to the hearts of her cousins, Abassur's beloved sisters. Glaïmir had to do little to cast into Nérillis' soul the bitter suspicions of his heart. Thus, that very evening, at the moment when Abassur, coming from the theater, returned home more intoxicated than ever with music, songs, and dances, his mother and sisters surrounded him to reproach him for deserting private and family life and pressed him to renounce those outside pleasures, while showing him Nérillis all in tears beseeching a look from her future husband.

In view of the sobs of Nérillis, pale and grown thin, Abassur's entire past came to mind. He recalled the intimacy of their naive love, the vows he had made to his well-beloved. He regretted the transports of his faculties toward the delights of art. He searched the depths of his heart and believed he still found there the same love for Nérillis.

The entreaties of his mother and sisters kept him at home the next day. That day, Elia sang only for the public; and the public was colder than usual in noticing the disquiet that seemed to flaw the voice of the much-loved artist.

The following day, there was the same absence of Abassur. That time, the women who performed with Elia were obliged to carry her from the stage. She had been faint before the end of the first act.

FOURTH CANTO

Abassur's family had required him not to appear at the theater or museum until the day of his wedding, for which the preparations were advanced. He, vanquished by the obsessions of his sisters, the tender solicitude of his mother, and the desperate looks of Nérillis, sadly prepared himself for the betrothal ceremony.

It was on a summer morning that those preliminaries to a more intimate union were accomplished. The family meal having ended and the two young people engaged according to the rite of the Tasbarite people, Abassur left his father's house and went toward the port. There he jumped into a boat rented to him by one of those marine ostlers who make a living by renting *talersis* for cruises; and, himself taking the cetacean's reins, he goaded it in such a way that the *talersis* soon made the boat fly along over the waves with all the speed of its fins.

Three suns assembled in the zenith shot forth burning rays from the blazing sky onto the lukewarm waves. Abassur directed his course along the shore in the direction of the extreme maritime suburb to the west of the city, and, avoiding the heat of the day, he went to seek shade and solitude in the midst of the *tarrios* forest, so well known to dreamers, melancholy souls, and misanthropes. He stopped a moment under the bough of one of those giant trees, the enormous trunk of which plunged down and took root in the sea's rocky bottom while lifting above the water a top with vigorous limbs feathered with large, green or garnet-red leaves.

Abassur was contemplatively gazing upon the undulations of the water driven back by the powerful breath exhaled from the *talersis*'s nostrils, when, upon raising his head, it seemed that, in the distance, he saw passing and disappearing among the trees the celestial and spiritualized form of Elia. A *Repleu* was guiding her *talersis*, which proceeded capriciously, describing circles between the dome of greenery and the moving waves.

Scarcely had the time of a lightning flash passed, when Abassur's *talersis*, pricked by the goad, bounded in the direction in which the apparition appeared. But before his craft had turned around in grazing several trunks supporting the canopy above the sea, Elia's image was lost behind the solid mass of a tree thrown down by waves. Abassur sailed for some time in the depths of the wood, searching on every side for Elia's shadow. In his mad eagerness, he struck the cetacean with redoubled blows. Exasperated and furious, the animal soon disregarded the hand of its guide; and, coiling its harness around the limbs of a *tarrios*, it broke its traces, escaped at complete liberty into the sea, and left Abassur immobile in his boat attached to the branches of the marine tree.

Abassur, mute with disappointed rage, disengaged his small craft from the bonds holding it fast and, taking his oars, sadly prepared to regain the shore.

At that moment, the skiff carrying Elia passed at some distance from him; and this time, Abassur could distinguish the features of the woman who had initiated him into the spirit's pleasures.

Flaousta the *Repleu* guided the *talersis* with a firm hand; and the prudent Vanoumi was reclining in the stern.

Elia, standing, her eyes fixed on the waves which in places mirrored rays filtered through the *tarrios*' foliage, seemed to be the sylph-queen of those somber and mysterious localities. The young woman's boat moved forward slowly. For the first time, Abassur was struck by the divine charms which the whole city of Tasbar had admired so long, but which he, cut off from carnal emotions, had seen only as living manifestations of art.

In that magical place and in that hour, after the ceremony which had come to put his future under obligation, Abassur could not think of the artist: it was the woman who appeared to him in all the glory of her gentle, sad, and supreme beauty. For the first tame, he noticed Elia's slender, aerial figure, that diaphanous and white flesh animated with an infinitely fresh pink, those features of the most angelic model, and especially the expression of that face, where goodness and tenderness disputed preeminence with nobility of spirit and intellectual power.

It was not given Abassur to contemplate Elia more than an instant, for without her having lifted her head or being able to perceive him, her *Repleu* had guided the gondola in another direction.

When the craft had completely disappeared from sight, Abassur, raising the veil over the state of his heart, perceived that, without suspecting it, he loved Elia. His soul tormented by regrets and disquiet, he beat his oars in the water and painfully regained the forest shore. A few moments later, he returned alone, his head bowed and face somber, through the western suburbs.

At almost the same moment, Elia, upon returning home, found Glaïmir awaiting her return with a face beaming with visible contentment. Nevertheless, he came, he said, to complain to Elia of her severity and of the obstacles she was putting in the way of the accomplishment of his happiness and of the projects he had formed so long before. He envied, alas, the situation of his friends of whom several were touching upon the realization of sweetly dreamed hopes; and, as an example, he mentioned Abassur's betrothal, which he had attended that morning.

At that news, Elia paled, but remained strong. She wished Glaïmir an affectionate farewell and asked him to leave her alone; then, accompanied by Flaousta, she went to the *abare* which six years earlier had carried her from Lessur. Elia had steered it rather often and knew the mechanism thoroughly. With all dispatch, she had her clothing and the instruments necessary to the practice of the arts put into it; and, before Ruliel had reappeared on the horizon, Elia soared up into the sky, accompanied by her two servants, Vanoumi and Flaousta.

It was not until three days later that Abassur learned of Elia's flight. But he told himself that an etheric navigator of his skill could quickly overtake the fugitive; and, without informing any of his relatives or friends, he himself equipped his powerful *abare*, which the Tasbarite people had nicknamed *The Eagle*, and mounted into space with the speed of lightning.

FIFTH CANTO

Abassur knew Elia's relations with Lessur too well to believe the young woman could have directed her course to another globe: therefore, he went straight to that satellite.

After a journey at galvanic speed, he landed on that world, where the breezes, charged with nuanced aromas and changing perfumes, caress nature while intoxicating it.

Our voyager's search had made him think for a moment he was on Elia's track. Meanwhile, he in vain traveled through the diverse countries with landscapes of sweet enchantment. He visited the cities, each view of which, apprehended as a whole, is a picture of grace and harmony. Also in vain, his feet trod upon fields where the flowers are so abundant that the eye nowhere can distinguish the earth they cover.

Despairing in the futility of his search, Abassur resolved to go as far as Elier, where Elia still had some relatives in her maternal grandmother's family. Here, also, Elia had been seen; her opaque *abare* had for a moment touched that world of crystal; her relatives had embraced her for half a day; then, she had departed again.

Abassur traveled thus several times from Lessur to Elier and from Elier to Lessur, never being able to overtake Elia. The dove sometimes would perch an instant on one of those islands in ethereal space and would take flight again.

Then finally, it happened that, after various peregrinations, Abassur no longer heard any word of Elia. The sylphid, doubtless, had made herself an inhabitant of the ether; the angel now wandered in celestial abodes.

Abassur, deprived of half his soul, dead to the moral life, resolved to deliver himself from the material bonds which tied him to earthly things. Elia having been lost, he felt within himself only one need—to die.

But it would have been beneath Abassur's great heart to dream of quitting life without making his death serve science and humanity. At first, he had the idea of returning to Star and attempting, like so many others, to penetrate into the center of Rêvour, through the phosphorescent atmosphere which covered it and veiled mysterious valleys. But, one day, when he was refreshing his fatigued lungs from the unnatural and seldom-renewed air of his *abare* by inhaling the fresh breath of Elier's zephyr, he seemed to recognize at one point in the sky, above Erragror, a luminous star which observation informed him was a comet, the frequent returns and changing forms of which had already tried the telescopes of astronomers on all the globes of the Starian system.

Abassur had some damage to his *abare* repaired and

himself helped supply it completely. That operation finished, he made the courageous resolution of shooting forth into the sky in pursuit of the comet, with the goal of inspecting at close range the transformations of its substance and of observing the phenomena which were taking place in its flaming atmosphere, though he might perish embraced by the projection of its fires.

The Eagle, with a strong flight, adventuring into the still unexplored regions which border upon Urrias' orbit, for two days plunged into the crimson rays of that star. At last, he disengaged himself with joy from that blazing circle of attraction and rose above the path traversed by the red sun.

The comet was only several thousand leagues from him! *The Eagle*, intensely electrified by Abassur, leaped over, devoured the sky, and, some days later, the comet offered itself like an immense earth encompassed on all sides.

It required all the competence and experience Abassur had acquired in the management of *abares* to follow with an equal speed the comet swept away into the Heavens. Abassur approached it closely enough to distinguish, by means of a telescope, the physical phenomena taking place in the luminous atmosphere and on the surface of the solid mass. Ten times the curiosity of the scientist, pushed beyond the limits of prudence by the lack of care he had for his life, was at the point of drawing upon him some bolts of lightning or, at least, blinding that eagle who did not fear to look upon a sun from too close.

His observations finished, Abassur stopped suddenly, his eyes still turned toward the comet, which he watched flee before him. He saw it become smaller and smaller, until the distance showed him nothing but a luminous point.

Death had not wished he who has tempted it; and Abassur, feeling himself henceforth destined to live for the success and greater glory of his nation, sadly took again the course toward the satellites of Star.

Already, the orbit of Urrias had been passed over at a point opposite to that which *The Eagle* had crossed it in its outward course toward the comet. The *abare* moved more slowly; and Abassur, his eyes wandering through bottomless space, successively brought back his thoughts to the five globes he knew so well—where he had many times visited the various countries, and where every beach had borne the imprint of his feet.

At that moment, an opaque and slightly luminous point appeared to him comprising, with the globes of the Starian system, a fifth satellite. That point was located below and close to him, as far as he could judge; little by little, it lost its phosphorescence in proportion as it approached and finally became, after several minutes of rapid motion, a small globe about three leagues in diameter.

Upon approaching more closely, Abassur remarked that the asteroid possessed an atmosphere of great purity and that at the surface of that little world, the vegetation rose from the soil strong and varied.

The Eagle, descending from space, came to throw itself down and to breathe in that refreshing air, greeting with joy the chance encounter of that oasis in the deserts of the Heavens.

Having secured his *abare*, Abassur, with curiosity and circumspection, plunged into the groves of those divine regions; he refreshed his palate at the brisk sources of pure brooks and tasted all sorts of fruits and other foods which the earth appeared to produce in uncultivated abundance.

The night having come, Abassur observed, a short distance from the hospitable little globe which he had come upon in his course, another asteroid of the same appearance, which gravitated at that moment not far from him; and he could not doubt that the heavenly space between Elier and Urrias contained several of those celestial bodies and that their smallness had prevented them from being observed previously by astronomers.

Abassur roamed for two days over the surface of the asteroid.

The morning of the third day, he set about climbing a small mountain the slopes of which were strewn with clumps of trees in flower. The rays of Erragror, which was rising behind that hill, tinted its summit with an azure dawn.

At that instant, a start which shook his whole being made Abassur jump... He had heard the divine sounds of a lute vibrating under a practiced hand.

He still knew nothing of the origin of those harmonies; nevertheless, running madly, he rushed forward and soon stopped, panting with astonishment and unquiet joy in seeing Elia standing at the very height of that mountain of enchantments...

But was it indeed Elia? Her head was encircled by the disc of Erragror as if by a celestial nimbus. The spiral curls of her hair, moved by the wind, shone intermingled with the star's rays. Elia made her lute resound with divine harmonies and seemed to command and preside as a goddess over the destiny of that enchanted planet, perhaps an Eden of the lower Heavens.

Alas! It was only the soul or the image of Elia transfigured.

Abassur, who in the first burst of joy had believed he had found his Elia, the artist of Tasbar, fell to his knees confused and overwhelmed... She whom he had loved was of the nature of gods or of angels!

SIXTH CANTO

The unexpected and fantastic apparition of Elia—radiating light, of aesthetic magnificence at the highest point on that enchanted world, which seemed to have been placed there only in order to serve her as a throne in the Heavens—had left Abassur on his knees moved by the divinity of the being who had kindled within him all the passions of spirit and of flesh. He remained in contemplation before that divine image. Doubtless, he suffered in seeing her as of an essence incompatible with his human nature, but he consoled himself by feeling within him the power—what am I saying?—the irresistible need to love her. Henceforth, he only wished to love her as a man may cherish his idol or his god.

Still, the blue sun, without ceasing to pour torrents of light upon Elia, transfigured at the summit of the mountain, was already rising to a degree from the horizon. For Abassur, Elia's face was thus disengaged from the nimbus the sun's disc had formed around her head. She ceased her harmonies and turned her divine eyes into space where Star showed its immense moon.

From that instant, Abassur's illusion began to dissipate. What he now saw of Elia reminded him more of the woman. This was indeed the spiritualized form which made the Tasbarites question whether Elia belonged to humanity; but the uncanny was dissolved for him.

The impetuosity of these emotions were drawing him to the feet of his dearly beloved when he saw a short distance away and coming in his direction, Vanoumi, Elia's faithful *Repleu*.

Restraining the enthusiasm of his heart, he charged the clever Vanoumi with preparing Elia for his appearance.

And, a few moments later, Elia, choking with happiness, hastened to throw herself into his arms!

Here began for our two lovers a delectable life, in which the needs of the spirit and the heart, poetry and love, found a blessed and delightful satisfaction. The asteroid with its enchanting wooded regions seemed to be the heavenly paradise assigned them by the god of celestial rewards so that they might enjoy the happiness which had seized them.

To Elia now belonged the great soul and powerful genius of Abassur.

Abassur, in love with the artist, in love with the woman, intoxicated himself with Elia's poetic inspirations, all in covering with kisses those pure features which had become his possession.

Such sensual pleasures are innumerable.

One day, however, Elia, whose eyes were following in space the revolution of the Starian world, recalled to Abassur the memory of his mother and sisters, who were pouring out tears over his absence or perhaps even mourning his loss. Only that thought could cause the two lovers to resolve to tear themselves away from the delights of their oasis; and, some time later, *The Eagle* brought them back to Tasbar.

A certain anxiety had pursued them during the time which the *abare*, in its vigorous projection, employed in leaping the distance. Abassur primarily dreaded the look of Nérillis. But he had said that their happiness would have no shadow. Upon their arrival at Tasbar, they found Glaïmir at Nérillis' feet. Their mutual suffering had brought them together; and, that day, the two young people, themselves engaged, were on the point of being married.

Abassur's return to Tasbar was not without glory for him. The report of his astronomical observations and daring discoveries spread throughout the world, and, although he was still young, the Chamber of Axiarchs extended the honor of calling him into its bosom.

For a long time, he lived with Elia, his beautiful wife; they were both admired and cherished by the Tasbarites.

Nevertheless, they sometimes returned into space and went to isolate themselves from the world on the delightful asteroid which had become their property and which now bore the name of Elia. For, alone, with poetry and love, in that Eden in the ether, they always recovered their former intoxication, which was like a foretaste of the pure happiness promised to the just in the superior stars of the Heavens.

THE END

EPILOGUE

THE WORLD OF DREAMS

O marvelous, strange spheres,
Lands where at liberty my thoughts in rapture
Have found extensive skies
To mold to their inclination conquered nature,
And by capricious spurts
Sowing a movement, a glimmer, or a creature—

You were the origin
Of my dreams. Star is one of those strange worlds,
Eldorado, Eden,
Which each of us adopts for himself and arranges,
Beautiful fields of the foreign
Which every mind invents and embellishes.

It is the better sphere;
It's riches to the poor, a fairy to children,
And to the Moslem dreamer
His paradise. It's better than expectation;
For one lives in spirit there,
There, in one's own world, in imagination.

In building cloudy castles,
In dreams I passed my earliest childhood leisure;
Days of indolent repose
Slipped away in dreams of the greatest pleasure,
In the most wonderful lives
Which childish pride embraced with gentle pressure.

Of old, was Star, then,
One of those castles of delicious candy?
No clarity, no precision
On that subject comes into my dim memory.
I wanted it all very fine;
And nothing has been adorned with so much fancy.

What does it matter!... My agile, adventurous spirits
Were bound to be pleased when they caught sight of this
  theme.
Nil novi sub sole: All since the Hebrew prophets
Have repeated these words... Now, let's create a realm;
And let's invent suns with more delightful planets:
To and something new, let's give light to them.

Well, now, as in the time
Of my daydreaming infancy,
My thoughts inhabiting
An immense dream ceaselessly,
Star appears, assuming
Form and reality.

REGENERATIVE HOPES

Fantastic worlds, where every soul in grief
Escapes with passion, would you, then, be the gulf
Where the surplus, the excessive nourishment
Of our dreams are lost? What! Could this ravishment
Outside of us, despite our inspired souls,
In the ruby Heavens, in the gilded spheres,
Be nothing but lunacy, imagination?
Myself, I'd much rather see the intuition
Among us of destinies which, in future eras,
Will send our soaring toward celestial shores
And will, at last, lead us in our migrations
From one globe to the next as so many stations
To the Heaven foreseen by the inspired soul,
Where humanity, transfigured and beautiful,
Will find voluptuousness, perfection, joy.
This noxious, obscure globe, where misery
Marches beside us, in the vast, cold spheres
Secluded, doubtless—on the scale of worlds—
Is the most inferior, the lowest.
Of its sustaining essences, the purest
Are already consumed. Each people who pass
Over its poor soil leaves, with their trace,
More impoverished fields and more arid ground.
Its leavens are already almost exhausted
Across the older of its two hemispheres.
So, are the strong peoples going to search for lands
And settle farther away? Man can yet
Secure the nourishment for his powerful flight.
But when, thus, by mankind each exhausted fraction
Of the reproductive essences is drained,

Will Mother Earth rebel and refuse to nourish?
Oh!... Humanity is eternal, and cannot perish!
Their inventive genius, before that great disaster,
For a new homeland will have chosen their star;
On a better world of the superior regions
Mankind will have concluded their migrations.

And even though, still, our feeble might
Up until then, vainly, will search for the insight
To travel through the Heavens... doubtless, there are
On nearby planets, some of those beings higher
Than us by their nature; surely there are on some worlds
Races of giants; and, finally, space abounds
In humans who, more perfect in body and mind,
Endowed with longevity, strong and bold,
Will, themselves, supply the question's answer.
We will see them come before the final hour
To give us the means of crossing the heavenly realms,
To find there the objects of our happy dreams,
And bring us, perhaps, to the vermilion spheres
To see Star more magnificent and richer in wonders.

FAREWELL TO THE READER

At this title, reader,
It seems to me I see you let slip a grimace!
Is it that our author
Wishes in concluding to give us his preface?
It would be here quite noble and good in its place.
It's at the book's ending, then, that it's recognized
And understood that an author is welcome indeed
To speak to us of himself. But I've no desire
To turn aside from the route I've followed here.
To the shafts of incensed critics
Enough other temerities
Will have exposed me. In a few words, however,
I can elucidate my thoughts on one point.
Dear reader, I don't expect
—Nor, perhaps, would desire—
To see all approve of *Star* and what it had
Of the new, the strange, the until-now uncreated.
I want you to comprehend,
Reproach and reprimands would not humble my pride.
Oh, under my task, indeed,
In my projects I have paused;
But I say that in this way it's good to stagger!
Under a great subject I bow almost crushed:
But what does that matter!
If I've done badly, I've attempted much.

*May these stories drawn from another world have made
you forget for a moment the miseries of this one.*

Defontenay.

237